D0804761

LOWELL PARK

A Historical Novel by Mike Chapman

Copyright © 2003 Mike Chapman

All rights reserved. No part of this book may be reproduced or transmitted in any form or by any means, electronic or mechanical, including photocopying, recording, or by any information storage and retrieval system, without permission in writing from the publisher.

Published, printed and distributed by:

McMillen Publishing.

A Sigler Company

Library of Congress Control Number: 2003111481

ISBN: 1-888223-53-7

www.mcmillenbooks.com

All of the opinions expressed herein are solely those of the author or subjects and do not necessarily reflect those of McMillen Publishing.

Cover photo courtesy of Alvah Drew.
Lowell Park photo on back cover courtesy of John Thompson.

Acknowledgements

This novel was born out of the deep affection I feel for history and for two of America's greatest Presidents. I am indebted to Bill Shaw, publisher of Sauk Valley Newspapers, for hiring me as executive editor in 1988 and bringing me to Dixon, Illinois, and the hometown of Ronald Reagan. Bill was a wonderful boss and loves the history of the Dixon area as much as anyone possibly could. I also am grateful to Joel Nagy for selling me his house, which sits just one-half mile from Lowell Park. That proximity caused me to become very interested in the history of the park and to develop the story line for the novel. John Thompson, the enthusiastic executive director of the Dixon Area Chamber of Commerce, has been helpful all along the way. His father and mother, Bill and Jean Thompson, provided me with many wonderful stories of the young Ronald Reagan and his summers at Lowell Park. And, as always, I owe a huge "thank you" to my wife Beverly, who believed in the story from the outset and has provided invaluable support.

Chapter One

– 1990 –

"Not again," mumbled Jennifer Brix as she raced her bike down the darkened street, her legs pumping furiously. She darted in and out around the numerous puddles caused by the freak summer rainstorm which had belted the area just two hours earlier. "I can't believe this is happening to me."

She maneuvered the sleek bike around several cars moving slowly down the street. Two college-aged men hanging out the window of a blue Mustang whistled as she whizzed past, but she paid no attention. As usual, she was behind schedule and had no time for such frivolities. The bike hit the curb hard, flying over it and onto a long sidewalk. Jenny coasted for a few seconds and then began pedaling as hard as she could again. She sped past several students on the sidewalk; one of them yelled at her as he leaped aside at the last moment to avoid a collision.

"Sorry!" she shouted back over her shoulder. She shook her head in frustration and cut a hard right, moving out onto a huge open field. In the dark, looming directly ahead of her, like the Sphinx out of the desert, was Schaefer Hall, home of the university's history and philosophy departments.

She braked to a skidding halt in front of the building, the bike almost falling to the ground as she leaped off. She jammed the bike into a parking spot and fumbled with the lock in the dark, securing it. She grabbed her backpack from the rack on the rear of the bike and raced up the steps of the building. Jackie Smith was waiting for her just inside the front door.

"Geez, Jenny. Don't you have any regard for time at all?" Jackie blurted out, glancing down at her watch for dramatic affect. "The lecture's already started."

"Sorry, Jack. It just got away from me," Jennifer shouted as she raced past, motioning for her friend to follow. "Did he really start already?"

Jackie nodded, then shrugged. She fell in behind Jenny, walking as fast she could down the long hallway.

"Yes, but I doubt we missed anything," she shouted ahead to her friend. "Professor Burns is old; very old. He doesn't get around too well. It probably takes him a while to warm up...."

They slipped into the large auditorium and stood at the back for a moment. There were several dozen students scattered about in the spacious auditorium, leaving hundreds of empty seats. They moved up front, pushing into a row of seats, past several male students. Two of them glanced up with bored expressions, then smiled widely at the two attractive co-eds. One of the men bumped the other, pointing up at the late arrivals.

Jenny and Jackie dropped into their seats, staring up at the stage. An old man, thin and frail with a shock of long, white hair, stood behind the lectern, speaking in a voice thick with passion.

"...that we should know more about the past leaders and heroes of our society. It is our solemn duty, as serious students of history, to pass the torch...to try and maintain the heritage of our nation. In order to do so, we must try to understand what it was that motivated these men and women to act as they did. We must try and understand their times, the conditions of their youth that impacted them, for that is how they became who they were. Environment is a huge key to understanding people, and history...."

Jackie leaned over to whisper to Jenny, her eyes glued to the stage.

"Look how old he is. He looks like he might die right here in front of us."

Jenny nodded, beginning to scribble in her notepad.

"He must be at least eighty years old," Jackie whispered.

One of the men sitting next to Jenny leaned over to her, placing his arm on the back of her seat.

"Hold it down, ladies; please. I'm trying to soak all this in....."

Jenny glanced at the notebook in his lap. The word "history 140" was neatly printed across the top of an otherwise empty page.

"I hope you didn't get writer's cramp from all those notes," she said, sarcasm dripping from each word. He frowned at her and removed his arm, slinking down in his seat. Jenny turned her attention back to the stage, listening once again to Dr. Burns.

"We have a responsibility to those who don't understand the impact of history, who don't comprehend its immense value, to lead the way. We must make every effort to pave the way for others to follow in our educational path."

He paused, glancing out over the sparse audience.

"I was a trailblazer once, but my time has expired. I am passing the torch to you...to all of you here tonight. The torch of caring about who we once were, where we came from as a nation. We need to remind younger generations what made America great, and what they need to do and be in order for the nation to continue to be great." He paused. "It is not an easy burden."

He paused again and coughed twice. He looks ill, worn out, Jenny thought, as he stared out into the audience, his eyes searching.

"Perhaps there is someone out here tonight who cares enough to make a difference. But you must care enough to live it...I mean, truly live it. Make a true commitment. Love it, caress it, and *live it....*"

Jenny sat spellbound. Somehow, it seemed as though he was speaking directly to her. But then, she always seemed to feel anyone talking about history was talking directly to her. She had a passion for delving into the past, a passion which at times bordered on obsessive, or so she had been told countless times by her friends, with Jackie at the head of the list.

As the hall emptied thirty minutes later, Jenny and Jackie eased their way toward a small group of people surrounding Professor Burns on the stage. Jackie had tried to talk her into leaving the moment he was finished, but Jenny was anxious to hear more of what he had to say and clutched her notepad and pen as she edged closer. He was talking in such a low voice that Jenny couldn't make out what he was saying.

Suddenly, the professor tensed, clutching at his chest with both hands. His eyes widened and he slumped slowly to the ground, in slow motion, almost as if he was acting. A startled hush enveloped the small group as two men loomed over him, horrified expressions covering their faces.

"Good lord! He's having a heart attack!" shouted one of the men, jerking his head around with desperation, glancing in all directions. "Help! Get help! Quickly!"

A portly woman screamed and a man raced off the stage, shouting for a doctor. Jackie grabbed Jenny's arm.

"Oh, my God, Jenny! He's going to die, right here in front of us," she gasped, eyes wide.

Jenny stared down at the professor, expecting to find him in a state of terror. Instead, he appeared calm. His eyes were now nearly shut, his lips curved in a faint smile. She eased in closer, her eyes glued to his face, her heart pounding.

"Has anyone called for paramedics?" shouted the man kneeling by the professor, cradling the head full of snowy white hair in his arms. Getting no response, he blurted out, "Does anyone here know CPR?"

Jenny swallowed hard and nodded. She knelt on the floor, next to the professor. She reached out her hand, touching the professor's hand. Dr. Burns's eyes opened and locked on hers.

She continued to hold the gnarled hand, gently stroking it, sensing that he was not as bad off as she had initially feared.

"He doesn't need CPR," she whispered to the man next to her, who was trembling as he stared at her. He obviously was very frightened. "He's coming around on his own."

Several moments later, the paramedics rushed in and took over, working hurriedly on the professor. Jenny stood and backed away, watching the proceedings silently. Finally, the paramedics lifted Dr. Burns to a stretcher. They carried him off the stage and from the building, out into the night. Jenny and Jackie trailed along behind, watching until the ambulance disappeared into the dark, its siren whining out an eerie melody.

"Wow, do you believe that?" croaked Jackie at last, turning to Jenny. "What a night. I think we need a beer or two, or more. C'mon, let's go to Dirty Jim's."

She grabbed Jenny's elbow, and acted shocked when Jenny gently pulled away.

"Not me," said Jenny softly. "I'm going home."

Jackie tried her best to talk her into going to their favorite hang-out, but Jenny knew they would wind up telling the story over and over and over, and she simply wasn't in the mood. She just wanted to go to her apartment and try and evaluate all that had happened, in her own way. She needed her space; and she needed Cid, too.

Jenny spent a tense night. At first, she couldn't find Cid, but he finally came moseying out from the back porch of the apartment. He was a tough-looking cat, mostly black with some small white splotches, as though an artist had shaken his paint brush and the white paint had stuck on the black fur wherever it landed. Jenny had been studying Spanish history at the time she found him as a sick and thinly stray wandering her neighborhood three years earlier. She had just finished reading "The Poem of the Cid" and immediately named him in honor of Spain's greatest warlord and hero, El Cid.

She had difficulty falling asleep, the memory of the professor's eyes etched in her mind. She finally drifted off and had a series of short dreams, each of them about death. She awoke tired, and stumbled off to the kitchen, picking up a stack of mail from the previous day. She reached into the refrigerator and pulled out a Diet Coke without even looking, then walked across the room, sipping at the drink, immersed in her mail.

It was a small apartment but well maintained. Her first four years of college she had tolerated a steady stream of new roommates. "It's the best way to meet people and form lasting friendships," her dad had told her over and over. But each semester had been a mini disaster; she had never been comfortable with any of her roommates, all of whom had far different interests than hers, and different agendas, as well. She had worked at various jobs in order to pay her way through school and couldn't ever seem to find the time to socialize to the extent everyone else seemed able to. She was in constant arguments with roommates over whether or not she was going to "loosen up" and "have a good time." School, her two part-time jobs and, of course, her working out — another obsession of hers, she truly did not understand how anyone could go through a week without at least six good, hard workouts — left her with precious little time for social activities.

When she began working on her master's degree two years earlier, she decided she had earned the right to some privacy. Now, nearing the completion of her advanced degree, she was even more convinced she had done the right thing. Though it was certainly more expensive to live alone, privacy was a luxury she very much enjoyed at this stage of her life. Cid was her only roommate the past two years, and they got along just fine together, each learning to give the other space when it was needed. She plopped into a chair, reading a letter from her mom. The walls behind her were full of photos and posters, but there wasn't a rock star or movie actor in the group. The photos of a dozen American presidents, ranging from a huge photo of Abraham Lincoln in her living room to a small portrait of John F. Kennedy in her study, adorned her walls. Even Richard Nixon and Herbert Hoover could be found somewhere in the apartment; though they were two of the most maligned presidents in recent decades, they were two she admired, each in his own way.

The doorbell startled her, and she almost resented it when she opened the door to see Jackie standing there so bright and early, wanting to talk about the excitement of the night before, and admonishing her for not going with her up town. Jenny hadn't even gotten in her six-mile run yet; Jackie knew how Jenny felt about starting off the day with a run but was too anxious to see her to wait any longer.

Jenny sat in the chair, bent over while lacing up her running shoes, nodding politely as Jackie rambled on and Cid rubbed against her leg. She was relieved when the phone rang and it was for Jackie. Her latest steady, a pleasant fellow named Mike, knew to call her at Jenny's if he couldn't reach Jackie at her own apartment, in the same building.

"Yeah, it was really weird," Jackie said into the receiver. "The poor guy was so old that you were afraid something bad was going to happen at any second."

Jenny looked up, frowning. Jackie glanced at her and covered the phone with her hand.

"What's that look for?" she asked.

"He *is* old, not *was* old," said Jenny. "He's still alive, you know. He's not in the past tense yet."

Jackie shrugged and returned to her phone conversation. She talked for several more minutes as Jenny began her limbering up exercises, getting ready for her run. The stormy night had passed and she saw through the window it was a beautiful day. She was anxious to run away the anxiety built up from the previous twelve hours.

"Hey, Jen...the phone's for you," said Jackie.

Jenny looked up, surprised.

"I didn't hear it ring..."

"Call waiting, remember? Hello, Jenny...this is 1990, not 1920 or 1930, where you spend most of your time these days, it seems." Jenny took the phone from her and propped it against her shoulder as she continued swinging her arms across her chest.

"Hello," she said, pausing. "Yes, this is Jennifer Brix."

She paused again, listening intently to the voice on the phone.

"He wants to see me? Why me?" A perplexed expression spread over her face as she listened to the voice on the other end.

"Okay. Sure. I'll be there. Give me the address again, please," she said, motioning for Jackie to hand her a pen and paper. "I don't know exactly how to get there."

She wrote quickly, then hung up the phone.

"So what's up, babe? Hot date with one of those jocks that are always chasing you, or something?" Jackie said. When she saw the expression on Jenny's face, she frowned again.

"Hey, what's wrong? You look like you're in shock."

"He wants to see me," said Jenny quietly. She leaned back in her chair as Jackie studied her.

"Who? Who? C'mon, tell me. Was it Todd Hill, that guy who hit on us — you, mainly — at Dirty Jim's? Who?"

Jenny stiffened slightly.

"Professor Burns. That was his assistant calling. The professor is in a room at the University Medical Center."

Jackie gasped with a mixture of shock and disappointment. She stood up, hands on hips, glaring down at her friend.

"So...you're not going are you? You don't owe him anything."

"No, of course I don't owe him anything," said Jenny, tucking her shirt into her shorts. "But, he kind of caught me off guard, you know? I said I would come...and now he's expecting me. So I'm going."

"You really are a dingbat, Jenny, you know that?" said Jackie. "All of the young guys on this campus that chase you and you spend all of your time thinking about old men like Ronald Reagan and Professor Burns. I hate to say it...but you're kinda weird!"

"I just happen to admire men of substance. That's all," said Jenny, peeved that her best friend had her on the defensive and that she felt the need to defend herself.

"Well, whatever turns you on, I guess," drawled Jackie. "As for me, I like men of...muscle. And of...."

"Yeah, I know!" said Jenny, interrupting with a chuckle. She couldn't stay angry with Jackie for more than a few moments. That was one reason they had remained close friends for so many years. Jenny viewed life in such a serious vein that it was good for her to have Jackie around to provide some balance and keep her based in reality. And to make her smile from time to time.

"We *all* know what turns you on, Jackie."

Jackie smiled and threw a pillow at Jenny just as Jenny grabbed her backpack and ducked out the door.

Jenny had never liked hospitals and had come to hate them ever since her father's quadruple bypass surgery six years earlier. She had never gotten over the shock of walking into the recovery room with her mother and seeing the white body lying there unconscious, with tubes sticking out of his nose, mouth and chest. He appeared to be dead, and her mother had almost fainted. Jenny had resented that the hospital staff had not prepared them more adequately for what they were to see. Her father had recovered, but the sight of him stiff on the table had never really left her mind. For someone concerned with health and fitness as she was, a hospital was a sober reminder of how fragile health could be. She felt an involuntary shudder as she walked down the long corridor to Room 12 E.

Facing the room, she stopped, and took a deep breath. "Why am I even here?" she asked herself. And then she entered.

Professor Burns was lying in a bed that was propped at a forty-five degree angle and turned slightly toward the window. He had the room to himself and the small television set was covered with a towel. There were several large bouquets of flowers from members of the university's history department.

She could see the outline of his face and he appeared to be sleeping. She glanced nervously around the room a second time, then bit her lower lip. She cleared her throat lightly and he turned toward her.

"Ohhh, there you are," he said in a voice more fragile than she had remembered. He looked up at her, his lean, craggy face wrinkling into a faint smile. "Please," he said, motioning toward the small chair by the bed, "won't you sit down?"

Jenny smiled self-consciously and sat on the edge of the chair. He stared at her so intently that she was forced to smile.

They began to talk at the same time…then stopped, chuckling lightly.

"You first," he said.

"I was just going to ask how you are feeling," she said.

"Better. Much better," he said. "Maybe this rundown, antique body has another few miles left in it, after all."

"I was really worried last night," she said, groping for something to say. "For a minute, I thought...."

"Yes, so did Dr. Morris. He was undoubtedly wondering about the notoriety the University would receive for killing off an old travelling professor in such an undignified manner."

"Oh no, I'm sure he was worried more about you than..." Jenny stammered.

"Then I'm afraid you don't know Geoffrey Morris very well," said the professor.

They both laughed lightly, but Jenny stopped abruptly. She was nervous and uncomfortable.

"Professor Burns, why did you invite me here?" she asked softly.

He paused, staring at her for a long moment.

"Because, I've been wanting to see you again," he said finally, his voice soft and low.

"See me again...since last night?" she asked.

"No...I mean, yes," he responded. "To thank you for the compassion you showed an old man. Holding my hand. Pumping some life back into this tired body."

"I was...very concerned for you," she said, searching for the right words. "When I saw you lying there on the floor, it was as if, somehow, we were...like friends."

"Yes, we are friends," he said.

"But we just met..." she said.

Professor Burns fidgeted with his nightshirt and looked over at the small table next to his bed. He reached for a box of tissues and wiped his eyes with a tissue. He looked back at Jenny.

"You are a lover of history," he said.

"Yes...but how did you know?" she asked.

"Why, you told me so, Jenny," he responded.

She felt a sense of exasperation. Maybe she shouldn't have come after all. She wished she had gone for her run; now she was worried if she would find time to squeeze it in before she had to be at the restaurant, for work.

"How? When?" she asked finally. "We'd never met, until last night."

"Nonetheless, I knew," he said.

She stood and stared down at him in the sterile bed, then glanced around the room before looking him in the eyes again.

"This conversation doesn't seem to be making any sense," she said at last. "Maybe I should leave. I...I must be upsetting you." Professor Burns looked pained and leaned forward in his bed. He reached out a wrinkled hand and caught her wrist. His grip was very soft, his flesh cool.

"No, no. Please stay. I only meant that you told me so by the very fact of showing up last night, to hear my lecture. A beautiful young lady like you must have many other options on how to spend her nights. And, since you came to the lecture, I know you must love history."

She felt suddenly relaxed. She smiled to reassure him she would stay, at least a bit longer.

"I'm always teased by my friends," she said. "To them, the world revolves around football games, bars and dates. It's not that I'm a prude, really it's not. But the truth is I've always been fascinated by the greatest men in history. Alexander the Great, Hannibal of Carthage...El Cid." She paused. "I even named my cat Cid."

He chuckled at that, a sparkle in his eyes.

"Conquerors and warriors only?" he asked, studying her closely, rejuvenated by her decision to stay longer.

"And thinkers, too," she hastily added. "Plato and Aristotle, Confucious; Benjamin Franklin. Thomas Jefferson and Abraham Lincoln."

He nodded, pleased at how the conversation was developing.

"Great men. Are there any other presidents, besides Mr. Jefferson and Honest Abe?" he asked, arching an eyebrow. "Anyone more...current?"

"Well...I've always been interested in Ronald Reagan," she said. "I don't understand him very well, but I'd like to. I'm not... certain we would hit it off, but I'd like to have met him, some time."

"In his presidential years, or even before that?" asked the professor, arching an eyebrow. "Perhaps as a young man, in his formative years; find out what really made him tick? Where all those ideals and firm beliefs came from?"

She smiled and nodded.

"Yes, probably back when he was a young man."

There was a long pause as the two studied one another. She felt a strange sense of attraction between them. She tilted her head and

16

smiled faintly. He nodded to her and a smile worked its way slowly over his lips. He was about to respond when a doctor and nurse entered the room.

"Company, Professor Burns?" asked the doctor, a middle-aged man. "That's good. A granddaughter?"

"No, heaven's no," he responded, sitting up a bit higher in the bed. "Just a friend. An old, dear friend." He smiled and winked at Jenny.

"We're going to do some tests now," said the doctor, walking to the side of the bed to read the charts. "You may want to wait outside, Miss."

Jenny nodded and walked to the doorway. She glanced back over her shoulder. The professor was watching the doctor intently and seemed to have forgotten her for the moment. In the hallway, she felt a slight dizziness.

"I hate hospitals," she muttered to herself. "I've done my good deed for the day."

She hustled down the hallway and moments later emerged out into the bright light of day. She felt strangely exhilarated and began to jog down the street.

Chapter Two

As the small, hard rubber ball flew toward her, Jenny leaped to the side, her body twisting as she swung hard. The tip of her racquet caught the tiny ball and sent it careening off the large white wall in front of her.

Her opponent, Bud Harper, grunted as he smacked the ball as hard as he could, sending it to the baseline with such power that she had no chance to get it before it bounced twice, winning him the final point of the game. They both slumped against the wall, sweat pouring off them, chests heaving with the exertion.

"Great workout, Jen!" he gasped, lifting a forearm to wipe the sweat away before it ran into his eyes. "I sure like playing you. You hustle. You really go for it!"

"That's the purpose of life, isn't it?" she said, voice cracking with fatigue. "Going for it?"

"It sure is with you. For many others — not so," he said.

"Well, Bud, you know I never wanted to be like other people," she said. "My dad always used to tell me, 'You get from life exactly what you are willing to put into it.' I thought it was just another of his corny sayings at first, but now I know he was right on the mark."

He smiled, and pushed off the wall, staring down at her.

"Let's go again," he said, gripping his racquet tightly. She pushed off the wall and moved into place, squatting slightly, gripping her racquet, staring at the blank wall again.

It was nearly seven hours later and pitch black when she pulled her bike up in front of the apartment house. A noise behind her stopped her in her tracks and she glanced sharply over her shoulder, into the darkness. She saw nothing and started up the steps to her apartment. She heard the noise again and spun around, looking behind her. There were several people walking some way down the street, but no one close by. Then a tabby-colored cat poked its head out from underneath the stairwell, glancing up at her.

"Buddy!" she blurted. "Always poking around, and scaring me." She walked over to him and picked him up, scratching his tummy, hugging him close. She turned to put him down…and saw a car sitting down the street, its headlights shut off but the motor running. It began to creep toward her; she watched intently as it slowly approached.

The car stopped in front of her house and the window in the back seat came slowly down. She stared into it and walked over, slowly.

"I've called you several times, but you weren't in," said Professor Burns, smiling up at her. "You left the hospital without saying good-bye."

She was shocked to see him, but was slowly beginning to realize she should not be surprised at anything that involved him.

"How did you get released so soon?" she asked, bending down to his level and peering into the car. He was wearing a thin, gray overcoat, with a scarf around it. He looked very warm. "And… aren't you hot, dressed like that? Geez, it's nearly eighty degrees still."

"They said I was okay to leave," he said with a shrug. "But they insisted I needed to keep warm." He laughed lightly and took the scarf from his neck and laid it down beside him in the seat. He looked up at her again, his eyes warm and friendly.

"I need to talk with you, Jenny," he said. "It is of the utmost importance. Will you come take a little ride with me?"

He opened the door for her and slid back to allow her space to sit down. She saw the driver up front look back at her. He opened the front door and walked around to the back door, standing by her. She gaped up at him. He was a large man, in his mid sixties, with a short, neatly-trimmed beard. She hesitated, then climbed into the

20

back seat. He glanced down at her without a trace of emotion, then shut the door, walking back to the front. He climbed in behind the wheel and the car pulled away.

"That's Brock, my companion," said the professor. "He's a man of few words, but very, very strong. I get tired on trips like this and he carries all the luggage and makes the arrangements. He is an invaluable aide."

"He looks...very efficient," she said, not knowing what else to say.

They rode for a few blocks without talking. Then he turned toward her in the seat and placed his hand on her hand. She glanced at him, and felt completely relaxed. Again, she experienced the strange but powerful feeling that she knew him very well.

"Where are we going?" she asked.

He smiled, patting her hand several times.

"Jenny, I want to give you a very special gift," he said. "I feel like...I owe you that."

"You don't owe me anything," she protested meekly, allowing him to continue holding her hand.

"More than you'll ever know," he said, with emotion. She gaped at him, puzzled.

"But Professor Burns...all I did was hold your hand...."

He laughed lightly and leaned back in the seat, eyes glued on her.

"My dear young lady; it was far, far more than that," he whispered. He uttered a large sigh before continuing. "Tell me, Jenny, what is your special field of study in your doctoral program?"

"It's just a master's program," she said. "I haven't decided on whether to continue into the doctoral program. Six years of college can get pretty expensive.

"But to answer your question, my field of study is American presidents."

He nodded, as if offering approval.

"Ah yes...we were discussing presidents at the hospital when we were interrupted, and you had to leave so abruptly. We didn't get to finish the conversation. I found it quite stimulating. I would like to continue it, if we might."

She nodded her approval; it seemed a small price to pay, if that was all he wanted.

"So...who is your favorite president?" he asked.

She shrugged.

"I guess it depends on how you define favorite," she said. "Like most people, I believe Lincoln was the most important, and did the most for the country. I can hardly imagine any other person being able to hold this nation together during the Civil War. It took an extraordinary man...to accomplish what he did. And then there are Washington, Adams and Jefferson, in the formative years." She paused.

"But didn't you say you were fascinated by Reagan?" he asked.

She nodded.

"He used to live in Iowa, if I'm not mistaken," he continued. "Worked at a small radio station in Davenport, then moved over to Des Moines for a couple of years to do sporting events. Why, he even used to broadcast some University of Iowa games, if memory serves me.

"But he was raised in a small town in Illinois, by a river," he added as an afterthought.

"Yes, Dixon, Illinois," she replied. "The Rock River runs through it. He mentioned it often during his presidency. He holds a special place in his heart for Dixon and the area he grew up in. He once said his goal was to make the United States the type of place that Dixon was when he was a youngster, back in the Twenties."

The professor chuckled.

"Sounds rather idealistic, wouldn't you say?"

Jenny shrugged again.

"I suppose it does," she said. "But that's the key to understanding Reagan. His passion for his youth, for the days he spent in Dixon, for a more simple world unfettered by huge, intrusive government. It was such a different era for America. He is idealistic and I admire that quality! I believe Reagan eventually is going to be regarded by historians as another Lincoln. Decades from now, he will be looked upon as a larger-than-life figure. A folk hero. Think of it — he even survived a very serious assassination attempt! If Kennedy hadn't been assassinated, I believe he would have self destructed in his second term. Like Nixon did in Watergate. Kennedy had so many skeletons...or, rather, women...in his closet. I think it would have caught up to him eventually.

"But Reagan — the attempt on his life made him even stronger, in both his own resolve and in the perception of the American people," she said, with a growing intensity.

"The man has lived a charmed life, no doubt," chuckled the professor, rubbing a thin hand through his hair.

"No! That's what everyone wants to believe," said Jenny, leaning forward and peering into his eyes. He could see that she was warming up to the discussion and it pleased him immensely. "But his life wasn't charmed, or even blessed. There was hardship and adversity. His father was a drinker, as we all well know, and the family moved a lot during his formative years. He simply became what he did through his own determination to overcome, and his overwhelming desire to become someone.

"Reagan had an insatiable thirst to be something special, to rise above the ordinary. I admire that so much..."

She leaned back in her seat as the car came to a halt. The driver leaned back and peered over his shoulder at his boss.

"We're at the park, Professor," he said, his voice low and thick. Jenny could not make out his features in the dark but she saw him nod at the professor. The professor nodded back.

"Thank you, Brock," he said. He turned to Jenny.

"It's a beautiful night and we have a lovely park before us. Will you walk with me a while?" he asked. She agreed and they stepped out of the car. They strolled along the sidewalk and then veered off the cemented path. He pointed toward a solitary picnic table, and they ambled over to it. He sat down heavily and looked up at her. She glanced about the park, then back at him.

"Look at that moon," he said, pointing overhead. It was full and bright, riding high in the sky. "Do you know what is so amazing about our moon, Jenny?"

She glanced up at it, studying it for a long moment.

"Well, it's a piece of compressed rock spinning around the earth at a medium distance of two hundred and forty thousand miles and...."

He chuckled, holding up a hand in protest.

"No, my dear. There's much, much more to the moon than cold, hard figures. Why, think of it, Jenny: the moon is the single most observed object in the history of mankind. Every single person who has ever lived — every man, woman and child who has normal eyesight — has seen the moon, since the beginning of time. You can't say that about any other object...not even the sun, because we'd all go blind looking at it for very long.

"But the moon...ah...Abraham, Moses, Gilgamesh of ancient Sumer...the heroes of the Iliad...Genghis Khan, Cleopatra and Julius Caesar! Jesus of Nazareth and Joan of Arc...George Washington and Abe Lincoln...Napoleon! Everyone who has ever lived has stared up at that very same moon, at one time or another. "It is the great common denominator for all of mankind."

She studied it for a long moment and then looked over at him, not sure what to make of it all.

"I've never thought of the moon in that fashion," she said softly. "It's...a wonderful concept, the way it unites us all, all of mankind. I like that image a lot."

They were quiet for a few moments.

"Life is too short for all of what we hope to accomplish," he continued. "It seems like just yesterday I was...was like you, Jenny. Young, full of vigor; eager to learn all I could."

"I believe what you said the other night," she said suddenly. "We must understand history. We must pass the torch... and there must be someone to accept it."

He nodded solemnly and sighed.

"Soooo...are you ready to...live history, Jenny? Would you have the courage to go back in time? I mean, if it were possible?"

She laughed and sat down beside him.

"I've often dreamed of doing just that," she said. "It would be so...terrific."

His eyes narrowed as he looked at her, and she felt the hair on the back of her neck stand up. She was suddenly nervous, in a strange way that was both intriguing and a bit frightening.

"What if you could, Jenny?" he asked solemnly. "I mean... what if you really could travel in time? Would you have the courage to try it?"

She looked deep into his eyes and shivered. She leaned back, shocked, and glanced about nervously. She saw two people far off in the distance, walking slowly and holding hands. She saw Brock standing by a tree thirty yards off. There was something about the way the professor asked the question that made it far more real than it should have been.

"What a silly question," she said. She paused. "You seem so... so...."

"Serious? I am, Jenny. Very, very serious."

He placed his hands on his chest, as if to restrain himself. He closed his eyes and breathed in deeply, savoring the night air. His lips parted, as though he was about to kiss a long-lost lover.

Then his eyes opened, full of a faraway look.

"Jenny...what if...what if...I told you I had been to Troy. That I had met Agamemnon and Ulysses, talked with Helen...seen godlike Achilles race across the windy plain. That I had been in the camp of the Invaders and had walked through the streets of Troy, in front of the palace of Priam…before the destruction?"

Jenny was stunned. She stared at him, leaning back. And then, she smiled, slowly and faintly.

"I would…believe you…I think, somehow," she muttered.

"Bless you for that," he whispered, his voice quivering. "For believing. But then, I knew you would, Jenny. I knew you would believe." He paused before continuing.

"I was there, at the gates of Troy, in 1186 B.C. Think of it… three thousand years ago! One thousand years before Christ. I walked through the camp of the Myrmidons and saw Achilles and Patroclus in their tent, sipping wine, talking of war…."

Jenny was mesmerized by the possibilities, true or not. She leaned forward again, breathing heavily in eager anticipation.

"What were they like? Achilles, Helen, Hector, Ulysses?" she gushed. She stopped herself in mid-sentence and gasped. She was shocked that she had been drawn into his dream world so easily, so quickly. For just a fleeting moment, she wondered what kind of a spell he was working on her.

He smiled at her, his eyes more alive than she had ever seen them, sparkling with excitement. Once again, his demeanor reassured her.

"Surprisingly…like you and me, Jenny. Not so different at all. Like the moon. It's the same now as it was then. They saw the very same moon we see. The stars, the sun…life…it's the same, then as now!

"Life is people, men and women who dare to dream and hope, and fight for the things they value. Back then, at Troy, it was honor and glory. Today, is it so different? Honor and glory…and money. That is what the leaders in our society strive for. Not the everyday masses, of course; for them it is just a matter of survival, going through the motions from day to day. But the one-tenth of one percent, those who want the most out of their lives…not to just merely exist, to go to work, come home, eat and retire for the evening, physically and mentally…."

They fell silent, each lost in their own thoughts. Then, he reached for her hands and held them tightly in his.

"Where do you want to go, Jenny?"

"Go?" she asked, tilting her head quizzically. She felt like he was seducing her with his words and his thoughts and she pulled her hands away.

"In time," he said. "I can send you anywhere you want to go. Anywhere at all. Think of it, Jenny!"

"What...Why...why...me?" she stammered. "What do you mean?"

"For what you once did for me," he replied, staring into her eyes.

"But it was nothing," she protested. "Honestly. I only held your hand...for seconds."

"No, you did more than that. Much more," he said, shaking his head slowly, the emotion pouring out of his eyes.

"Listen, even...if... if...I did believe, how...."

"I have a machine, Jenny," he said. "A time transporter. It is very simple. Not the theory behind it, of course; but the travel itself. You merely...sit...and go...."

Jenny moaned and fell back against the back of the bench, bringing her hands to her head. She held her face for a moment, gently shaking her head. She looked at the old man, who was watching her closely, confused and shaken.

"How can I believe such a story, Professor Burns?" she whispered. "I like you a lot, but...this just...just isn't reasonable. It isn't really happening, is it?"

He held up a hand, smiling at her, and nodded.

"I know, I know. It was the same with me, many years ago," he said. "I just couldn't believe...until I took my first trip."

"To Troy?" she whispered, afraid that she might be moving into an area she might not be able to retreat from easily, or without considerable pain. Did she want to encourage him, to make him think that she could possibly accept this ridiculous proposal of time travel?

"Yes...but what does it matter," he sighed, leaning away from her and letting her hands go free. "You don't really believe, do you?"

When she didn't respond, he stood and looked down at her. He shrugged and began walking toward the car. After several moments, she stood and walked behind him in the dark, the stars twinkling overhead.

Brock was now leaning casually against the hood, watching. He moved quickly to open the door for them, then shut it after they were securely inside.

They rode in silence, each on their own side of the back seat.

Jenny stared out her window and up at the moon, watching it slip in and out from behind clouds. Somehow, it seemed much different to her than it had just an hour earlier. She turned to look at the professor, who was gazing out his side of the window, a weary expression on his face, his shoulders sagging. He looked like he had aged ten years in the last few minutes.

The car stopped in front of her apartment. She started to climb out, then felt his hand drop on hers.

"If you want to meet your hero, young Mr. Reagan, in Dixon, Illinois in 1932, Jenny, you must decide soon," he said softly but sternly. "I will pass you the torch, but only if you have the courage...."

She slid out of the car and stood alone on the curb as it pulled away into the night. She walked slowly up the steps and unlocked her apartment door and stepped into the dark room. She turned on the light and saw a white piece of paper on the floor. Jackie had shoved a note under the door saying she would be at Dirty Jim's. She placed the note on a table and walked to the window, looking out into the night. Slowly, she turned away...and found herself staring at the wall with a photo of the young Ronald Reagan in a lifeguard suit staring back at her. She walked over to it, running her eyes over it for a long time.

She gasped and jerked suddenly, looking down. Cid was moving against her leg and she leaned down to rub his back. The cat purred and looked up at her. She picked him up and walked over to the sofa, settling into it. She stroked Cid gently, her mind far away, full of stunning thoughts. At last, she leaned her head back against the sofa and kicked off her shoes. Then she shut her eyes.

The sharp ringing sound startled her. Cid was gone. She realized she had drifted into sleep. She had started to dream and was confused, half awake and half asleep. She rubbed her eyes, then walked to the phone tentatively, lifting the receiver.

"Hey, Jen? Is that you, hon?" came Jackie's high-pitched voice. There was lots of noise in the background. "Did you get my note? Listen, I'm down at Dirty Jim's with Mike. Todd Sherman is here. He came up and asked me about you. Jen, better get your buns down here. I think he's got the hots for you."

Jenny didn't respond, scarcely listening to her best friend, her thoughts elsewhere. She felt like she was still caught in a dream-like state, her mind leaping back and forth from the present to the past.

"Jenny? Hey, are you there?" came the voice.

"Oh, sure," Jenny said finally. "Listen, Jackie, thanks, but... but I don't think I can make it tonight. I'm...I'm thinking of going on a little trip. Could you...come by each morning and look in on Cid for me? I may be gone for a couple of days."

"What? Jenny, what's wrong with you?" shouted Jackie, clearly exasperated. "I told you, Todd Sherman is asking about you, and...."

Jenny hung the phone up and stared at it, fighting for her breath. She backed away slowly, then shuffled into her bedroom. She grabbed her small workout bag and jerked open a dresser drawer and sifted through it, selecting a few pieces of clothing and stuffing them into the bag. She pulled on a blue, short-sleeved sweater over her pink tee shirt, and then faded jeans over her blue shorts. She pulled her favorite running shoes out of the closet and set them down by her bed. She walked into the bathroom.

She picked up a tube of lipstick, applied some, and then jammed it into her bag. She picked up a toothbrush, giving her mouth a good washing. She slipped the toothbrush into the bag, too. She started to leave, but turned back to gaze into the mirror. Her long brown hair splashed off her shoulders and she reached back with both hands, pulling it into a ponytail, fastening it with a band.

"Jenny, old girl...are you cracking up?" she mumbled into the mirror. "Are you nuts...or...."

She walked back into the living room and stood before the phone for several minutes. She finally picked it up and dialed the phone number the professor had given her. When she heard his voice, she caught her breath.

"Okay, professor," she said firmly. "I'm calling your bluff. I'm ready to take the torch."

She listened for several minutes while he talked to her, arranging where to meet the following day. She scribbled some notes on a pad as he talked and then they hung up. She scooped up Cid and carried him into the bedroom with her, hugging him tight. She stumbled onto the bed and sprawled over it on her back, placing her hands behind her head as Cid lay on her abdomen, purring.

"Cid, old pal, I'm going somewhere very, very special," she whispered to the cat. "I believe in the professor, somehow. I...I really think...he can send me back in time. At any rate, I'll find out when we meet tomorrow."

After several long moments, she reached over and clicked on the radio. It was set on her favorite station.

"…glad you're with us again for another great night of golden oldies," came the crackling voice. The deejay chattered on then introduced the next song.

"Here you go…one of my favorites from way back when… the 1950s, sung by the Pony Tails, it's called *Born Too Late.*"

Jenny stared up at the ceiling as the words rolled over her.

"I see you walk with another, I wish it could be me…oh why was it my fate, to be born too late…."

She sighed and drifted off as the radio played on, the only light in the room the time on her digital clock. Soon, she was fast asleep, dreaming like never before in her entire life….

Chapter Three

The large black truck rambled down the highway with Jenny, Professor Burns and Brock all crammed in the front seat. It sped over the Mississippi River and turned east on Interstate 88, angling up from the Quad Cities. An hour after crossing the Mississippi, they passed a highway sign that read "Dixon, hometown of President Ronald Reagan," and Jenny let out a big sigh, shifting in her seat once again. Brock frowned, glancing at the professor, who smiled at him then turned to Jenny.

"Nervous?" he asked her.

"No. I'm just not used to sitting still for such a long period of time," she said. "Thank heaven we are just about there. How far is Lowell Park from downtown Dixon, anyway?"

"Only about two miles," said the professor.

The truck slowed to twenty-five miles per hour as it moved into the town one hundred miles west of Chicago. The city was founded in the 1830s by a frontiersman the Indians called Father John Dixon and was now the home of nearly sixteen thousand persons. They passed under a large arch that said "Dixon," and the professor pointed out the Nachusa House on the left. It was empty now, but in 1932 it was the best hotel in town, and where she should look for a room. The truck rolled down the busy highway that split the town in half. Within five minutes of entering the town on the east , they were headed out of town on the west side, after crossing over the gentle-flowing Rock River. The truck turned right at the outskirts of town and headed out Lowell Park Road, a beautiful drive at that time of year. Several deer standing alongside the road darted quickly away as the truck sped by. A family of raccoons ran quickly across the road; Brock slowed the truck to give them ample time to reach the safety of the ditch.

"Stupid animals," he mumbled. "Always out on country roads trying to get hit!"

Two miles north of town he glanced to the right. A large wooden sign with the words *Lowell Park* greeted them. He slowed considerably as he turned into the park entrance. They drove past a small welcome center on the left and immediately were in a thickly-wooded, beautiful park full of towering trees all huddled close together.

"Ooohh, this is gorgeous," breathed Jenny, leaning forward to stare out the front window. "Who would have guessed such a lovely park existed right here, so close to town."

As they rounded a bend and came upon an overlook, the professor motioned for Brock to pull over. The truck halted and they stared out over the immense park. They were at a large clearing in the road and through the treetops they could see the Rock River meandering far below. The entire area was so thick with trees that visitors almost forgot they were in modern-day Illinois. All three climbed out of the truck and walked to the thick stone wall that came up waist high on them. Jenny placed her hands on it and leaned forward, the gentle breeze stirring her hair. The professor stood back, watching her closely, a half-smile playing on his lips.

"I almost feel...like I'm back a hundred years ago," she said quietly. She surveyed the land, drinking it all in, savoring it. "Everything looks so peaceful way down there.

"I love it! Have you ever been here before, Professor?" she asked, turning to him. He nodded.

"Yes, but not for a long, long time," he said.

They climbed back into the truck and continued the descent to the floor of the valley. It was a long, winding drive down, but they finally broke into a flat open space. Four cars were parked near a small boat ramp and several men stood fishing from the shore. The Rock River flowed serenely by.

"See that?" said the professor, pointing to a stone building on the left of the road. It looked like it had sat in the same spot untouched for a century or more. "That's the old lifeguard house, where Dutch Reagan changed when he was working here in the late 1920s."

Jenny nodded solemnly, staring at it until they were long past. She felt a slight chill down her back, almost as though the building was watching her too, and she hoped the professor hadn't noticed. She glanced at him sideways and saw that he was focused on the road ahead, lost in thought, his hands knotted together in his lap, very intent. She wondered for the hundredth time what sort of fool's mission she was on.

The day after her phone call, he had spent hours with her discussing the physics and dynamics, hardly any of which she could understand. He called the time machine a transporter, and explained he had been involved in its development all along the way. He had first entertained the idea of time travel over half a century ago, he told her, and had worked with five scientists to make the dream a reality. He wouldn't tell her where the financing came from, but hinted the research had cost close to a billion dollars and was sponsored by a philanthropist who himself had traveled in time once, before dying.

He had come alive with enthusiasm, gesturing as he talked, telling her of his three time trips. He went first to Troy, then to ancient Uruk, the Sumerian city where the great king Gilgamesh had ruled some four thousand years ago. Lastly, he had visited Philadelphia in early July of 1776 to witness the birth of the United States of America. He had one final trip planned, he told her. It had taken him a long time to get up the courage to tell her, and then had only briefly.

"Ask me no questions, for I won't say any more than this," he said sternly. "I am going to Galilee, some time around thirty-three A.D."

His voice trailed off and he seemed lost in a daze for several long minutes. She had finally gotten up and left for a while. When she came back, he was at a large table with the drawings of the transporter, looking over the details. He was very pleased to see her again and pulled her to the table, going over the machine in great detail once again.

"There is one part you must remember, above all else," he told her sternly. "We have found the trip can only last for a total of eighty hours without the body starting to react negatively to the strain. Eighty hours. That's all. If you stay longer, you can not come back without great risk.

"Time travel in itself is relatively simple," he told her. "The theory is surprisingly easy, relatively speaking, once we stumbled across it. But the trip itself…is difficult on the physical makeup of the body. We found with some surprise that the human body begins to adjust to the new time zone and it is very difficult for the body to make the return trip after a certain period of time. We have set the safe limit at eighty hours…just three and a third days." He paused, looking at her.

"We have had…several travelers…who were not able to come back," he said quietly. "They were forced to remain in their new time zone, forever."

He reached into his pocket and pulled out a watch. She looked down at it, intrigued by the strange appearance. It was like no watch she had ever seen.

"Take it," he said, handing it to her. "As you can see, it is quite different from your ordinary watch. It was developed especially for us…for time travelers such as you."

He leaned forward, placing a bony finger on the front of it.

"Look closely, Jenny. It shows eighty hours on it," he said, tapping the glass top. "The last two hours are in the red zone, alerting you to departure time. You need to keep a very careful eye on the watch."

She shook her head slightly, still staring at the watch.

"Eighty hours…from when I arrive in the past?"

"No!" he said emphatically. "It doesn't matter what you do when you arrive in the past, as far as the eighty hours are concerned. All that matters is – that you return to 1990 within eighty hours of departure from this time zone. Your trip is based solely on this time zone, not on any other.

"Remember that, Jenny," he said. "It is all-important!"

She regarded him solemnly.

"Look, don't worry so much about me," she said finally. "I can handle this, honest I can." She paused. "But I'm worried about you. Are you okay? Where are you going to stay while I am gone for these eighty hours?"

He sighed deeply, relaxing. His eyes caressed her.

"Don't worry about these old bones," he said. "Brock has found an excellent motel room for us in Dixon. I plan to rest a lot while you are gallivanting about in 1932."

She recalled the powerful conversation as the truck turned off the main road and bounced gently along a seldom-used vehicle path. Then, Brock turned off that path and into a grassy area filled with large trees, twisting the truck around and past several behemoths. After two minutes, he braked the truck and stopped it. They were in a very secluded area at the back of the park. They all climbed out and Jenny stretched hard, looking around as she did so.

"We must wait for dark before setting up," said the professor. "Brock, make sure the transporter is fine, please."

Brock disappeared toward the back of the truck.

Though it was late in the afternoon, the air was sticky with humidity. There was a serenity about the place; Jenny glanced about again, feeling almost lonely…as though she had already entered a different time and place.

"It is beautiful here…but it's also kind of eerie," she said softly.

The professor nodded.

"I used to come here often, but it's been such a long time," he said. "Still, it's beauty never ceases to impress itself upon me."

She was surprised.

"You came here? To this exact spot?" she asked.

"I like the solitude," he said, walking several feet away. He looked down at an old path he was standing on, then looked up, as though searching for something. "There used to be an old hiking trail here. And over there…about two hundred yards away, is the Rock. You can barely see it through the trees."

Brock reappeared, rubbing his hands together, wearing a satisfied expression.

"Everything looks fine," he said. "Now, we just have to wait for dark."

Only the sound of crickets and an occasional bird call interrupted the silence of the park. From a goodly distance, peering through the foliage, they could see the last of the cars drive slowly past their spot, followed shortly by a park ranger truck. They were well hidden from view and the park ranger was not looking hard enough to spot them, anyway. There was seldom trouble of any kind in Lowell Park.

The professor nodded to Brock, who disappeared behind the truck again. He lifted up the back door of the truck and climbed up into it. He pulled out a long metal track and sat the end of the track on the ground. He went back into the truck and emerged moments later pushing a large platform on the track. It slid down easily. A heavily constructed chair, looking almost like a throne, sat on the platform, with a huge control center in front of it, attached to a long cylinder. He eased the platform down the track and set it down on the ground. He began to hook up a vast number of wires and gadgets, into complex energy devices which sat in the back of the truck.

"It will take Brock about two hours to set up," said the professor. "That means about 11 p.m. we will be ready. While he is setting up, let's review the procedures."

Jenny smiled faintly. He reached out an arm for her. He hugged her briefly.

"Now, do you remember everything?" he said gently, peering into her eyes. "We have you set to arrive at five in the afternoon... several hours before day's end. Time travel works best if we can avoid the intense heat of mid day, but we want you to have a couple of hours of daylight before night sets in so that you can get oriented and find your way. There will be plenty of opportunities to get into town; once you get to Dixon, look for the Nachusa House hotel. That's where you can stay.

"Again, there is no pain, but you will experience a slight dizziness. You may be somewhat discombobulated when you first wake up. Give yourself time to adjust, Jenny. Stay in the chair. And remember first and foremost...eighty hours is all the longer you can stay on this trip. Your watch is essential; keep it with you at all times. Go past eighty hours, then...you can't return. And money. You will need some cash to help you. I have one hundred dollars, all in small bills issued prior to 1932."

He handed her a stack of bills, most of which she folded and stuck into her bag, now slung over her shoulder. The rest she stuffed in her jeans, forgetting in the excitement of the moment that she already had several one dollar bills in there.

"I'm so anxious that I'm not even frightened," she said. "A bit tense, perhaps but that was to be expected. We have covered the procedure so thoroughly. I am confident that there is nothing that can go wrong." She shook her head then, giggling.

"What…is this, really?" she gasped, pressing her hands to her head, as though to confine and control her thoughts. "I can hardly believe this is all happening to me!"

Two hours later, the moon was riding high overhead when all three stood by the transporter, staring intently at it. The entire platform was twenty feet by twenty feet and four feet high, with two little steps leading up to the top. The hefty chair was solidly positioned on the platform, with a series of very thick tubes leading from it to the large cylinder facing the chair. The cylinder had a large, black-faced center with bright orange numbers, dates and figures all over it. The entire cylinder was two feet wide and was ten feet thick. All of the dynamics for the trip were hidden deep within its chambers, like a giant super-computer.

"It's time, Jenny," the professor said softly, his eyes glistening with emotion. He dabbed at them with a hanky. Jenny took a deep breath and climbed up the steps and onto the platform. She settled into the large chair, her small bag in her lap. Brock strapped her in tightly with one long brown belt while the professor went over the time dial one last time, bent over and touching it delicately with trembling fingers. The rustling in the trees gave them all a´start, and Brock jumped off the platform, heading toward the bushes. A deer leaped out of the bushes, stood alert and tense for a moment, then darted away. Inadvertently, the professor's fingers bumped the dial, just a bit. They all laughed nervously.

The professor straightened up and reached for a piece of paper in his pocket. It was folded neatly four times. He handed it to Jenny.

"Here, this is a message for you when you arrive in 1932," he said. "Don't look at it now. It's simply a small precautionary bit of instruction that will help you. Study it when you get a few moments, but within the first couple of hours."

She smiled faintly and took the paper, stuffing it in her pocket, next to a portion of the bills he had given her earlier.

"You are about to embark on the most fascinating journey any human can make, Jenny," he said, backing away, his voice tinged with emotion. "How I envy you...."

"How long...did you say it will take?" she asked nervously. "I've forgotten already."

"Only two minutes…one hundred and twenty seconds, once the transporter is activated," he replied. "But remember, you will be very tired when you arrive in 1932. Time travel is very tough on your system, a tremendous form of jet lag, if you will."

"Jenny?" he croaked, asking if she was ready.

She sighed heavily, then: "1932…here comes Jennifer Brix!" The professor nodded at Brock, who leaned over next to Jenny and gripped the lever. She gaped at him, her hands gripping the edge of the chair so tightly that her fingers tingled. He pulled the lever just a bit and a whirring noise began. Jenny's eyes widened in eager anticipation. Brock looked at the professor, who gave him the go-ahead nod. Brock pulled the lever back further. The machine began to vibrate slightly.

"Ohhhhhhhh…I…feel…light-headed," Jenny gasped, turning to the professor.

"It's fine, Jenny. Fine," he shouted.

"…but my…head; I'm…going…to…pass...."

The transporter emitted a high whining noise and quivered slightly. Jenny jerked twice and then her head slumped to the side, eyes shut. The transporter began to fade from view…and then suddenly it disappeared. The silence was shocking to the professor and Brock. They gaped at the spot where the machine had sat just seconds before, both fighting for breath.

"Damn! That's the sixth time I've seen it do that, Professor," gasped Brock. "And I still don't believe it!"

"I don't believe planes can fly, either, Brock," said the professor, his shoulders slumped, suddenly exhausted. "It simply defies logic. But I've been on them…and they do indeed fly. And…this machine does indeed fly, as well. It flies through time…just like a 727 flies through air."

They walked slowly back to the truck and slipped into their seats. The professor looked back at the sight where the machine had sat only moments ago.

"Oh, how I envy her," he whispered. "But, time travel is for the young." He sighed, and paused. "We might as well try and get some sleep. We want to be well rested when she returns."

Chapter Four

The transporter began to reappear, until it was back in full view. The whirring stopped and Jenny sat slumped against the back of the chair. She woke up slowly and began to glance about, disoriented. She rubbed her eyes, stifling a yawn. Everything appeared much the same as it had moments earlier, except the woods were thicker and the grass much longer. She sat still for several minutes, then released the belt. She stepped out of the chair, tucking her bag behind it. She moved slowly down the steps and stood several feet from the platform. She looked about her, surveying the scene very cautiously. Her legs felt wobbly; she lifted first one, then the other to her chest, pulling on her shin, limbering up.

"Pro...Professor Burns?" she croaked, surprised at how her voice sounded. She cleared her throat and tried again, louder.

"Professor Burns...where are you?"

The silence grabbed her and sent a chill down her spine. She felt terribly alone and strangely vulnerable. She wrapped her arms around herself and shivered once. She ventured a few more steps away from the platform, glancing all about her. She heard birds in the distance and looked up at the hazy sun. It was already low in the western sky and then she remembered she was going to be arriving in 1932 at 5 p.m. She also remembered the piece of paper the professor had given her and she stuck her hand in her pocket to find it.

"Hello...anybody?" she called out, much louder than before, as she fished for the paper.

A cracking noise behind her caught her attention and she pivoted, staring into the undergrowth, withdrawing her hand from her pocket. She scanned the forest and thought she saw movement. Maybe two or three figures were there, moving slowly. She raised her hands to her face, suddenly very nervous. If someone is in there, she thought, why aren't they answering me?

"Hello? Is anyone...there?" she shouted.

There was more quiet movement around her. She heard soft footsteps. She was beginning to grow a bit angry, frustration replacing some of her fear.

"Now, listen, I know you're out there. I don't feel like playing any foolish games," she shouted, hands on her hips.

A terrifying scream ripped the air. Jenny shrieked as a near naked man emerged out of the foliage, brandishing a large tomahawk. Jenny stumbled backward, hands flying to her face, gasping. He was lean and dark skinned, naked from the waist up, but wore a long loincloth. He was angry looking and had streaks of white and red paint across his face. For a fleeting moment, she thought he might be an Indian.

He shouted again, shaking the tomahawk. She quit thinking: she simply turned and ran as fast as she could.

She tore through the brush, glancing back over her shoulder. There were four wild men chasing her, all with painted faces. They screamed words she couldn't understand. Terrified, she ran wildly; branches struck her face and she almost fell once. She leaped over fallen logs and continued racing for her life. Her years of fitness training and hard workouts served her well, though she had no time to ponder that fact now. She glanced over her shoulder again and saw that they were falling behind.

She turned back...and slammed headfirst into a tall figure of a man, almost knocking him to the ground. He groaned and staggered back several feet as she bounced off to the side, tumbling to the ground. He gawked down at her and she gaped up at him as she came to a sitting position.

"Who the dickens are you?" he shouted, in a high-pitched voice.

"Behind...me! Wild men...," she gasped, turning to point in the direction she had just come. He glanced up and frowned heavily as he saw the wild men slowing down, having spotted him as well. "Ezra! Jeremy! Fire!" he shouted, picking up his own long rifle off the ground, where he had dropped it after Jenny ran into him. A volley of shots rang out and Jenny looked behind the tall man to see seven more men. They were firing long muskets at the wild men behind her. She turned and watched the wild men dart off into the forest. "That'll do 'em, boys. Good work," he shouted. He turned back to Jenny. He reached down for her, grabbing her arm and half lifting her off the ground with one swift motion.

She gaped at him, head spinning. He was about the same age as her, she guessed, but very tall and lanky. The strength of his grip told her that he was a powerful man, much stronger than he might have appeared at first glance. His huge hand gripped her elbow tightly. She stared up at him, numb with fear. Suddenly, he smiled, and she felt her fear begin to evaporate.

"You okay, ma'am?" he asked, his voice deep and soothing. "What are you're doing out here, all alone?"

"Those men…who were they? And why were they dressed like that?" she gasped, pushing the long strands of hair back from her face.

"Shoot, ma'am…they were from Black Hawk's tribe. Sac and Fox, I reckon."

He scratched his head with a big hand. "They always dress… like that. That's how injuns dress."

"Injuns?" she gasped. "What do you mean…Indians?"

Three other men, all young and gawky, ambled over, staring at her. They all wore dirty blue jackets with silver buttons, and scraggly gray pants. All were toting long rifles which looked like old muskets.

"Who…who are you?" she gasped, stepping back.

"Militia, ma'am. Illinois volunteers," said the tall man. "C'mon, let's get you to camp."

He clutched her elbow gently and they trudged off into the forest. Jenny walked beside the tall man, gaping up at him, trying to get a good look at him. He had a long, angular face. He was not handsome, but noble looking. A dirty white shirt with long sleeves rolled up to his elbows covered his torso. He wore long, dark pants and thick, brown boots. He carried the musket easily, his huge hand gripping the entire trigger guard.

They marched for nearly thirty minutes, her asking once where they were going and he lifting a finger to his lips, admonishing her to silence. Finally, they broke into a small clearing...and she saw the Rock River in front of her. There was also a small camp of sorts, with small canvas tents, a cooking fire and spit, and several sentries, men dressed just like the man who walked at her side. The first sentry gawked at her, scratching his head as she moved past.

"Jeosophat! What you got there, captain?" he mumbled in a twang she couldn't recognize. "We heerd the shots...."

"Don't rightly know yet, Samuel," said the tall man at her side. "We gotta get a better look, now that we're out of the woods."

The men around the tents stood slowly, staring awkwardly at Jenny. There were forty in the camp. There were five lots of rifles stacked together. In the distance, by the river, several horses and mules were tethered to a line between two trees

Jenny gaped at them, glancing around.

"Who... are you people?" she asked. "A band of gypsies?"

"No, ma'am," said the tall man. "Like I said...militia. Illinois regiment. I'm the captain here."

Jenny was at a loss for words. She didn't even know where to begin.

"Is Ronald Reagan here?" she asked, not knowing why she asked such a question.

"Don't reckon I know that name, ma'am," the captain responded. "Did he sign up recently?"

"Well, he's from Dixon, and...."

"Nope. No soldiers here from Dixon's Ferry," he said, shaking his head and leaning on his rifle, studying her. "We're part of the fourth regiment of Colonel Thompson, from down south mostly, near New Salem."

He led her to the campfire, where a slab of venison was already cooking on a spit for the evening meal. He bent down and sliced off a strip of meat with his knife. He grabbed a tin plate, slapped the meat on it, then added some beans from a nearby kettle and offered the plate to her.

"Hungry, ma'am?" he asked politely, shoving the plate towards her. "It's not really supper time yet, but we ain't eaten anything all day long."

"No...I...but, thanks," she muttered.

The men crowded up, looking at her with befuddlement. They were all young men, some little more than boys. The captain took the plate she had rejected and stuck his knife into the meat, and took a large bite of it. He chewed for a moment, still eyeing her closely.

"Small band of Black Hawk's men saw her first," said the captain to the men gathered around. "Gave her a goodly fright. But, she runs good. Real good."

The men chuckled, but fell to staring again.

"Ma'am, if you don't mind me asking, just what were you doing out here in these wilds?" the captain continued. "Why, Black Hawk himself could have nabbed ya."

Jenny was shocked and totally confused.

"Black Hawk?" she gasped. "You mean…the chief of the Sac and Fox?"

"Well, he ain't really a chief," said the captain, handing the plate to another soldier. "Keokuk's the main chief. Black Hawk is more of a war leader. But, he's got the power of a chief nowadays. He's pretty crafty, they say, and a good fighter. The others follow him and look up to him as a great warrior."

"Probably would have scalped ya, ma'am," said Ezra, inching in closer to stare at her. He paused as she looked at him in shock. "No offense...."

"Ezra, mind yourself. That's no way to talk to a lady," said the captain.

"Didn't mean no harm, captain. But…how'd she get way out here, anyway?" asked Ezra.

The captain stared hard at Jenny, trying to size her up. She sensed he was a kind, compassionate man and she felt no fear of him at all. And yet she needed to guard her secret about the transporter until she knew more about them.

"Ezra's got a good question, I guess, ma'am. As captain of the militia, I should know how you happened to be out here in the woods. Any other folk with you?"

"No…not really," she said. "I'm alone."

"If that don't get all," grunted Ezra. "Why, even Daniel Boone wouldn't go wandering out here by himself. And this lass goes and does it."

"Ma'am? I…don't get what you mean," said the captain.

She paused, then offered, "I'm…a traveler."

"From where? Going where?" he asked, with a frown.

"From Iowa City. And…going to…Chicago."

"Ioway? Shoot, ma'am, that's real wild country," said the captain, scratching his dark hair. "On the other side of the Mississippi. How did you get way out there in Ioway?" he paused again. "And where the heck is that other place...Chicago? Never heard of it."

Jenny bit her lip. She was beginning to realize she had gone a lot further back than 1932. She wasn't sure how to proceed, what to say. They would certainly not understand if she tried to tell the truth. They might even think she was deranged and needed to be locked away. She needed some time to think this situation through clearly.

"Oh...I feel faint. Can I sit?" she asked, biding for time.

"Yes, yes, of course. I'm sorry I didn't think of your well being," said the captain. He gripped her arm gently and guided her to a thick bedroll, between the fire and the river. She sat down on it, and he stood over her. She looked up at him.

"You rest now. We can talk more later," he said.

A sudden commotion in the forest caused all the men to drop to a knee, leveling their rifles. The captain stood by Jenny, protective, hand on his rifle, staring into the forest. A sentry called out... and an answer came back in English.

Two men emerged from the forest, dressed in buckskins. They talked briefly with the sentries, who pointed at the captain. The two men marched straight to where the captain and Jenny were. The first man, very rough looking with a thick stubble of beard, glared at the captain.

"You in charge here?" he asked in a growl.

"Yep," replied the captain, standing firm.

"You're Abe Lincoln, from New Salem village?" the man asked.

"That I am," said the captain.

Jenny let out a shriek and all three men turned to look at her. She gawked up at the captain, hands over her mouth, astonished by what she had just heard.

"You okay, ma'am?" asked the captain.

Jenny couldn't respond. She was too stunned to do anything but stare up.

"Who in tarnation is she?" asked the newcomer.

"We found her in the woods," said the captain.

"Doing what?" the newcomer asked.

"Running, mostly," the captain responded. "She's real good at it, too."

The newcomer turned back to Lincoln, his eyes narrowing.

"My name's Paulson, from down Peoria way. I'm a captain.

I'm taking over here, Lincoln. I have the rank."

"The way I see it, we're equal," said Lincoln. "Both captains. We'll share command, Paulson."

Paulson shook his head defiantly.

"Nope. I'm in charge."

Lincoln paused, rubbing a hand over his craggy face.

"Well, now, this needs some thinking on," he said. "I'm not so sure...."

"Tell you what, Lincoln," Paulson said. "I'll grapple with ya. Best man, why he's in command."

The others crowded around, eager for a contest. Lincoln smiled slightly and rubbed his jaw even harder. He regarded the man, much shorter but very thick and powerful looking. Then Lincoln nodded his acceptance. Several whooped in delight. A wrestling match was always a big attraction and welcome relief among the soldiers.

"Show him how a rail splitter wrestles, Abe," shouted Ezra, slapping the captain on the back as he began to limber up.

The two men swung their arms back and forth a few times, eyeing one another. The soldiers formed a small circle around them. Jenny stood, eyes wide, trembling with excitement, her head swirling with wild thoughts. Ezra noticed her and moved next to her, smiling.

"Don't worry none about the captain, ma'am," he said. "He's a durn tough country grappler. Lot stronger than he looks. He'll toss this fellow like a sack of corn."

"I know," she said. "I've read all about his wrestling exploits and his big match with Jack Armstrong back in New Salem."

She stopped abruptly. Ezra looked at her strangely.

"Read? About Abe?" he mumbled. "Tarnation! His set-to with Jack, even?"

"I mean...," she began.

She was saved from further explanation by the match. It had started. Ezra turned away, leaning forward in excitement. Lincoln and Paulson circled one another cautiously and then Paulson rushed in. He wrapped his thick arms around Lincoln's waist, securing a bear hug. He pulled in with all his strength and Lincoln groaned with the pressure.

They struggled in the fading light of dusk. Lincoln finally wedged his arms down inside the other man's arms, then wrapped his arms around the waist of Paulson. They were now locked in each other's bear hug. They teetered back and forth, groaning and scuffling. Twice they almost fell, but managed to keep their balance. Jenny was the first to see Abe slip a long leg between the legs of Paulson, and then hook his leg behind Paulson's left knee. They teetered again for a moment and then Lincoln pushed forward in a strong, sudden movement.

They fell heavily to the ground, with Lincoln solidly on top. Paulson groaned loudly, the breath knocked from him. Lincoln had him firmly pinned to the ground.

"Had enough, Paulson?" gasped Lincoln, staring down into the man's face.

"Yea…yeah!" Paulson mumbled.

Lincoln stood up and offered a hand to Paulson. The man hesitated, then reached up for it. Lincoln pulled him to his feet, where they stood face to face.

"You're a good man, Paulson," he said. "A scrapper. I like that."

"Same to ya, Lincoln," growled Paulson, shaking his head. "I'll be proud to serve with ya. And...to follow your lead."

"We'll split command, like I said," offered Lincoln. "Get something to eat, if you'd like."

Paulson shrugged his shoulders. He walked back to his companion and they moved off to the fire, where the others soon joined them. Lincoln brushed himself off and was about to walk over by the fire when he noticed Jenny still staring at him. He gave her a smile and walked over to her.

"You okay, ma'am? You look like you just been bit by a rattler," he said.

She struggled to find her voice.

"Are you really…Abraham Lincoln?" she finally whispered.

"Last time I checked, that was the case," he said with a shy grin. "But it's certainly not a name worth bragging about."

She swooned and he reached out for her, catching her. He held her awkwardly for a moment, until she regained her composure and stood back up. She slowly pulled away from him, eyes wide, and brushed back her hair.

"This is…unbelievable!" she croaked. "I go looking for Ronald Reagan…and find Abraham Lincoln! What…is going on? Is this all a wild dream?"

Lincoln shrugged again, looking confused.

"Sorry, I don't know this Reagan fella you talk of," he said. "He's not in the fourth regiment, that's for sure. Is he someone… special to you?"

"Oh, very, very special. A lot like you, Mr. Lincoln," she said, her voice trembling with emotion.

"Mr. Lincoln? Shoot, I don't reckon anyone's ever called me that before," he grinned. "Just Abe will do fine, ma'am."

She shook her head.

"Just Abe? I...I don't see how...I can call you Abe," she groaned. "I...I really don't."

She wanted to talk more, but she was growing very weary and the captain sensed she needed rest.

"Listen, no more talk for now," he said. "It's been quite a day already. Let's get you something to eat and then some sleep. You'll be fine, down here by water's edge. The men, they look young but they're good soldiers."

He walked away from her, pausing once to glance back over his shoulder. He motioned for her to follow and she hustled up behind him. They moved down by the river. Now, she was ready to eat something and he commanded the cook to fix her a plate. She ate the meat, some beans and a stiff piece of hard bread, washing it all down with cool water. She watched as the men prepared camp for the night, bustling about and chatting among themselves, all of them glancing at her from time to time. She thought fleetingly of her bag tucked behind the chair on the platform and wished she had it. Her thoughts were abruptly interrupted when Lincoln walked over to her again, and squatted down beside her, a long piece of thick grass between his teeth.

"This is not the fanciest place in Illinois," he said, forcing a faint smile. "But at least it will be safe for the night. You can have my tent."

He gestured toward a tent in the center of the small camp.

"There's two blankets in there...one to place on the ground and one to cover yourself with, when the chill hits the air," he said.

She remembered that the professor had told her she would be very tired from the trip and now fatigue was hitting her hard. The trip, combined with the sudden appearance of the Indians, the hard run and the incredible shock of meeting Abe Lincoln had her totally exhausted. She watched as Lincoln unrolled the thickest blanket and spread it out inside the tent. He motioned for her and she came to the tent. He stooped low and walked outside and stood back as she slipped past him into the tent.

She thanked him and he nodded at her, smiling again to reassure her. He then ambled off, looking back at her. She sank to the ground, sitting on the blanket, hunching her knees up to her chest and wrapping her arms around them. She stared out through the tent opening, glancing over the camp, trying to understand all that had happened in the past several hours.

Is this…real, or is it some type of elaborate dream, she asked herself. Is the professor really able to send people of his choosing back in time or is he a master illusionist, she wondered. She couldn't take her eyes off Lincoln; she watched him as he moved from man to man, talking briefly, several times glancing her way, the others peering at her as well. She knew she was the primary subject of conversation. She wanted to stay awake all night, to just watch, and watch and watch. But her body wouldn't let her. She slowly began to surrender to the fatigue, both mental and emotional, that was working on her.

She lay down, staring up through a wide hole at the top of the tent at the stars that were just starting to appear. She searched for the moon, but couldn't find it. She wanted to see the same object that the professor was looking at…somewhere, somehow, in another time yet in the same place. She imagined Achilles and Helen of Troy looking up at the moon, and Gilgamesh, and everyone else in the long parade of history. It was like counting sheep, only much more fun. The last thing she remembered was the image of Ronald Reagan, as a young man, looking at the moon, too…perhaps in this very spot, in another time….

Early the next morning, Professor Burns sat nervously at a picnic table, staring at the location where he had last seen the transporter. He was startled, suddenly, to see a young man jogging along the seldom-used path. The jogger saw him, too, and waved as he moved past, flashing a big smile. The professor hesitated and then waved back, watching him disappear into the thick forest. He was so surprised to see someone on the path that he didn't even hear Brock approach.

"You look worried, Professor. Is everything okay?" asked the big man, frowning at his boss. He had grown so accustomed to guarding the professor that he could quickly sense when he was concerned about something.

"I don't know," said the professor. "I made a mistake, Brock. A big mistake. I just now caught it when I was in the truck checking the transporter dial."

"A mistake?" asked Brock. "What kind of a mistake?"

"The timing was off on the transporter. It's coded by numbers, with a naval standard for time. Instead of 17-06-22-1932 it reads 17-04-22-1832. Just two numbers are wrong, but it's a difference of nearly one hundred years. We sent Jenny back to 17 o'clock on April 22, 1832, not to June 22, 1932."

"Holy cow!" gasped Brock. "How could that happen?"

"The time gauge on the dial was moved somehow," he said, a trembling in his voice. "Perhaps I...I juggled it when the deer came out of nowhere. I don't know for certain. It's as simple as that. Like when a faulty oil seal worth ten dollars stops a two-hundred million dollar space shuttle from performing properly. I just now saw it. I guess I was too excited last night to catch it."

"What does that mean?" asked Brock, a note of real concern in his voice. He was not a man who showed emotion easily, but he was growing fond of Jenny and was worried about her.

"It means...she's smack dab in the middle of the Black Hawk War. It took place all over northern Illinois in 1832, and in this very area. They were really just a series of minor skirmishes, with no major battles. Black Hawk's warriors were on the run most of the time. But there is the potential of considerable danger if she should fall into the wrong hands."

"What can you do about it now?" asked Brock, glancing about.

"Nothing," said the professor, his shoulders sagging. "It's all up to Jenny. She knows how to adjust the machine, if something goes wrong. We spent hours going over the details. And the note I gave her just before she left explained what to do with the time transport dial, if something went wrong. It was a last precautionary measure I needed to take, after we lost two travelers in 1975. If they would have had directions with them on how to reset the transporter's time dial, they would have made it back, I believe."

He paused.

"She's on her own now...but she's a very bright young lady. Yes, she is," he said, nodding his head vigorously, as if to reassure himself. "Yes...she is!"

Brock sighed and sat down beside the professor and they both stared into the thick woods.

Chapter Five

A splashing noise awakened Jenny with a jolt. She sat up
with a gasp and crawled to the front of the tent, eyes darting back
and forth over the scene in front of her. She saw a burned-out campfire, with three young soldiers squatting in front of it, sipping
coffee from tin cups. Down by the river, two soldiers were
fishing…and one had just jumped into the water. He was splashing
around wildly in his britches and shouting about how cold the water was as the others watched, laughing. She rubbed her eyes and
turned in every direction, gaping at the scene.

"Ohhh…I wasn't dreaming," she mumbled to herself. She
caught her breath and leaned back on her hands, mesmerized by
what she was witnessing.

Ezra walked out from behind a tent carrying his musket, but
she did not see Abe anywhere. She struggled to her feet, surprised
at how weak she felt, and stumbled out of the tent. Ezra saw her
and smiled, walking over to her.

"Mornin', ma'am," he said, tipping his hat slightly. He was a
gangly, unattractive sort, but he was at least friendly, she thought.
"Sleep okay?"

"Yes, good morning," she replied. "Where…is Mr. Lincoln?"

"The captain? Oh, he's out looking for Black Hawk. We got a

report his band of warriors crossed over the river last night and is prowling around this side somewhere. But, the captain told us to keep an eye on you," he said.

"Captain also said to make sure you got some food. He reckoned you'd be mighty hungry this morning."

She nodded at him. He walked to the fire site and spoke to one of the men. The second man immediately scampered around with a plate, fixing it with food from a large kettle and from a pan that sat on a wooden table. He glanced at Jenny while he worked, with a toothy grin. She nodded back and smiled faintly. Ezra took the plate and a tin cup and brought them to her. She peered at the plate, not sure what was on it.

"Here's some catfish. And some special fried tatters," said Ezra. "We was hoping to have eggs, but couldn't find no chickens this morning." He grinned at her, bowing slightly.

"Thank you," she said. "Ezra, isn't it?"

"Yes, ma'am," he said, taking off his hat and brushing back some bushy hair. "Corporal Ezra Smith, that is."

Jenny sat on a nearby stump and began to eat. She was famished and found the food tasty, if not delicious. Ezra watched her with fascination, as did the other men still working around the campsite. When she was done, he took her plate and dashed back to the kettle and returned with more. She thanked him and finished that portion off, as well. Ezra plopped down on a nearby stump, watching her intently.

"Where are you from, Ezra?" she asked, setting her plate down on the ground and sipping the coffee, which was terribly strong.

"Down Salem way. Near Abe's place," he said, with a touch of pride. "We been friends a long time."

"How long have you know Mr. Lincoln?" she asked.

"Nigh on to…two years, reckon."

"What's he…like?" she asked, tilting her head, smiling again. She was beginning to enjoy Ezra, and found him easy to talk with.

"Like?" he asked. "What do you mean?"

"Is he pleasant to be around? No, that's dumb. I mean…do you think he'll ever amount to much in his life?" She shook her head at the silliness of that question, as well, and took another sip of the coffee.

"Oh, shoot yes," said Ezra. "Why, Abe, he can do about anything. He's smart. Real smart. I imagine he'll be boss of his own store some day. Maybe even a general store, with lots of stuff for sale. Or maybe even be a lawyer. He talks about that, sometimes. He likes to read, though I can't see why myself."

Jenny laughed at Ezra's expressions.

"How about politics?" she asked.

"Abe? Politics? That would be real funny," said Ezra, slapping a palm on his knee. "Abe don't know nothing about that sort of stuff. He's too honest to be a politician." Several others had straggled over to listen to the conversation and they chuckled, too.

A series of shots rang out in the forest. Instantly, Ezra jumped to his feet and ran off with the others to the forest's edge, their muskets shoulder high and leveled at the trees. They peered straight ahead; Jenny came to her feet, hands on her face, staring after them, into the thick forest.

Several more shots rang out, followed by a blood-curdling scream. The men looked at one another, and Ezra glanced back to Jenny, as if to make certain she was all right. The branches of several trees rustled wildly and Lincoln and three other soldiers broke into view.

Jenny ran to Lincoln, who saw her and smiled widely.

"Mr. Lincoln...are you okay?" she sputtered.

"This 'Mr.' talk again," he said with a frown that quickly broke into a wide smile "The name is Abe." Then he paused. " Okay? What does that mean?"

"It's a colloquialism which derives from...oh, never mind," she said. "Did you see Black Hawk?"

Lincoln nodded, turning back toward the forest.

"Yep, from a distance. But that was close enough."

"What was the shooting...and that scream?" she asked.

"They shot once at us, then someone let out a war whoop, guess that's what you heard. We shot back and they scattered."

He walked down to the river, Jenny trailing along behind him, staring at him. He knelt at the water's edge and washed his hands. There was a small amount of blood on them. He stood back up, wiping the hands on his pants.

"Is that...Indian blood?" she gasped. "Did you wound someone in a battle?"

Lincoln chuckled.

"Hardly, ma'am. I cut my hand on a rose bush. Darn things are sure sharp."

She smiled at him and suddenly felt very self-conscious about the way he was looking at her. She strolled away, along the river.

He followed and they walked for a while in silence. She stopped and turned to face him. She was struck by the stark simplicity of his features.

"I just realized, I don't even know your name, ma'am," he said. "It's Jennifer. Jennifer Brix," she said shyly. "But everyone calls me Jenny. Or Jen." "That's a pretty name," he said. "Uncommon, but it suits you real fine." He paused, giving her a good looking over. "But tell me, Jenny Brix, why are you here? There is something...very odd about you." "Well, Abe...I like that fine. Being called odd," she said, folding her arms across her chest.

His face turned crimson. "Now, I didn't mean odd in a bad sense," he stammered. "No, ma'am. Why, anything but. Just...different. Like those clothes. And those shoes. I've never seen shoes like that."

He bent low, looking hard at her shoes. He lifted one foot of Jenny's and she almost lost her balance. She placed a hand on his shoulder to steady herself. He inspected the shoe carefully, then set her foot down. He straightened back up and she removed her hand from his shoulder. It had felt like a rock. He was lean and hard and very strong, she suspected from swinging a heavy axe regularly for years during his youth.

"What kind of shoe is that?" he asked, scratching his shaggy head of black hair.

"Asics," she said. "They're good for running."

"They proved that last night," he said with a chuckle. "You really outran those injuns. But those shoes kinda look like fat moccasins."

He paused again, his eyes narrowing.

"But I am still wondering, though, why you are out here, Jenny. It's sorta my business to know, as I'm headin' up this scouting regiment."

"Well, it's like I said last night, Abe...I was travelling. I am travelling. To Iowa."

"Last night, you said you were from Iowa, travelling to some place called Chicago," he said. "I don't know of that place. Unless I misunderstood you, Jenny."

"Yes, that's right. To Chicago," she said somewhat defensively.

"But you can't be all alone, Jenny. Not out here, in Indian territory. Why, your folks wouldn't allow it. Or your husband...if you have one."

She smiled at the last question.

"No…no husband. And parents, they…they want me to travel, see the world," she said and then paused. She felt a twinge of nostalgia mixed with regret. She had considered calling her parents before leaving with the professor but had decided against it. After all, she had wondered, how does one tell her parents she is going to take a trip through time?

"They wanted me to learn all I can. Why, when I graduated, they sent me to Europe, and…"

She halted, seeing the way he was staring at her. He was obviously confused and perplexed.

"To Europe?" he said, lifting an eyebrow. "That's really something. I've never known anyone who's been overseas. That's a long voyage, about twenty days, I reckon."

Jenny sighed, long and deep.

"Mr. Lincoln…Abe…can we forget about me for the moment?" she said. "I'll tell you more later, honest I will. But, it will be very, very difficult for you to believe me, when I do."

"No, it won't be difficult, Jenny," he said, with a shake of his head. "I'll believe you."

His expression was so sincere that she sighed again. She walked several more steps along the river, then turned. He hadn't followed, but he was watching her intently.

"Abe. Please, tell me about the war," she said, anxious to change the subject. "Why are you fighting Black Hawk and his warriors? What have they done that is so wrong?"

Lincoln walked up to her. He looked across the river into the forest and then back at Jenny. He towered over her, at six foot, four inches to her five foot, four-inch frame.

"For no good reason, sad to say. Black Hawk's a good man, a decent man, I reckon. He's fighting for what he holds most dear — his land and his way of life. Land to grow corn on and hunt on, and rivers to fish in. But, progress…it just won't be denied. The United States is young and eager to grow. It's gotta come this way."

She nodded to let him know she understood.

"Destiny," she said.

"Yes, I guess you could say that," said Lincoln. "But I admire Black Hawk, even if they claim he is breaking his promise to never come back east of the Mississippi again. They say he signed some sort of treaty years ago, but he claims he had no idea what it meant at the time. I wish we could convince him to stay out west in Ioway, and to give this land up without a fight."

"I don't think that will happen," she said softly.

"No, I don't reckon it will."

"And so, you will fight with him," she said with a slight shake of her head.

Lincoln reached down and picked up a long stick, turning it over in his hands.

"Well, it ain't me personally, it's the War Department. Those fellas in Washington who make the policies. I'd like to just scare him, if I could. That's why we sortie out every morning. Fire a few shots. Make some noise. As of yet, he don't have enough warriors to really go to war. But, he's gaining in numbers every day. He's been down to the Prophet's village, south of here, looking for recruits. We hear he's after the Winnebagoes and Pottawatomies, too. Our time's running out. General Whiteside is supposed to be headed this way soon and then things will get real serious, I'm afraid."

Ezra walked toward them, clearing his throat and looking sheepish.

"Captain, I think we should be moving on," he said. Careful not to make eye contact with Jenny so as to appear he was on official business. "Make a new camp. Black Hawk might be planning an attack some time soon."

"You're right, Ezra," said Lincoln. "Let's keep him guessing what we're up to. Tell the men we're going two miles upstream."

Ezra turned and left and she soon heard him begin issuing orders to the men. They began to pack up their gear, mumbling and joshing with each other as they worked.

Jenny looked around nervously, biting her lower lip.

"Abe…can I stay with you and your men?" she asked. "I don't know where else to go."

"We sure can't leave you alone out here," he said with compassion in his voice. "In two days, we'll send some men to Dixon's Ferry, about five miles downstream, for supplies. You can go along. Until then, you're more than welcome with us."

He paused and a sly smile came over his thin lips.

"Matter of fact, ma'am, I think the men rather enjoy having you here."

It was Jenny's turn to blush. And then, impulsively, she threw her arms around Lincoln and gave him a big hug. He gasped, staring down at her, and grinned. She backed up, dropping her arms.

"Sorry," she mumbled. "I'm just so…happy to be here. This

is…beyond my wildest dreams. Who could ever have imagined? I mean, Professor Burns…and Jackie…they would be stunned, floored, flabbergasted.…"

Lincoln scratched his head again, looking puzzled.

"Those names…flabber…flabber.…"

"FlabberGASTED!" Jenny shouted. "Isn't it a great word?"

"Flabber…gasted!" he managed, and then nodded. "Yes, that's a fine word. But…what does it mean?"

But Jenny's thoughts were already somewhere else. She glanced off in the direction of the time transporter.

"Abe…I just thought. I need to go…somewhere," she said. "Somewhere very important."

Lincoln held his hands up, palms toward Jenny, and shook his head.

"It's not safe to venture out of camp," he said sternly.

"It's not far," she said, her eyes begging for understanding. "But I really must go back to where you found me last night. You need to take me, though. Abe, please."

Lincoln was undone by her expression. He stared at her hard and then smiled faintly.

"We'll go along with you," he said with a sigh of resignation. "You sure can't go by yourself."

Jenny was pleased, but knew she could not allow Abe or his men to see the transporter. They would be shocked; they might even think she was a witch or a demon from another world.

"Surely, the Indians are not around now," she said. "Your shots must have frightened them off."

"Black Hawk's main party is still across the river, that's true," he countered. "But he has scouting parties on this side. The group that chased you last night, they're still around. We saw them this morning. And now, Black Hawk himself is here. Something must be going on."

Jenny walked in a tight little circle, hands on hips. He watched her with amusement, finding her very charming…and very attractive. Several of the other soldiers had been trying to listen to their conversation and were watching as they worked on their gear. More than one young soldier was already developing a fondness for her. She stopped and peered up at Lincoln.

"Okay. You can take me where I must go," she said. "But then, I will need some privacy. Some time alone. Please, Abe."

"I understand," he said.

57

An hour later, Jenny, Lincoln and ten soldiers moved along a thinly-marked trail. The men were keenly alert, muskets poised. Ezra was in the lead, with Lincoln next to Jenny. Suddenly, Ezra lifted his hand for them to stop, then gestured frantically for them to get down. They dropped behind thick bushes, hugging the ground. Jenny stared at Abe, who was looking straight ahead, a solemn expression on his face.

They heard faint noises. Then, six Indians broke into view. They were lean and well muscled, carrying bows. They moved swiftly, within thirty yards of Jenny and the soldiers. The Indians disappeared into the dense undergrowth as quickly as they came. After several moments, Ezra stood back up and motioned for them to follow him.

Within a couple of minutes, they were back at the clearing.

"This is where we found you yesterday afternoon, Jenny," Lincoln said, glancing all around. "How much time do you need? That war party might double back any time."

"Not long. I just need to be alone, Abe. I hope you understand," she said again.

He nodded solemnly. She moved away, into the surrounding trees. She heard birds chirping; it all seemed so peaceful. It took her several minutes to find the transporter. It was sitting back in the cove of trees and seemed to be exactly as she had left it. She climbed onto the platform and checked for her travel bag, relieved to find it was still there. She picked it up and pulled out the toothbrush, running it over her teeth thoroughly, wondering how people could have existed prior to the invention of the simple device. She set the bag back down behind the chair and checked the various switches, to make certain everything was in working order.

She looked at the time dial and then gasped. She leaned forward, staring at it. It read 17-04-22-1832.

"April 22, 1832? Good grief! Off by almost one hundred years," she mumbled. "What happened?"

She remembered the paper the professor had given her just before leaving and pulled it out, unfolding it. She read it slowly. She looked up, shaking her head.

"Great! He anticipated something going wrong with the dial, apparently." She sighed and began tinkering with the dial. "So…if the time dial ever happens to be wrong, this is what you have to do to fix it, he says.…"

She leaned over, sticking the paper back in her pocket, working with the dial. She maneuvered it to 14-06-22-1932. Then a sudden noise behind her caught her attention.

"Abe, you promised," she said as she turned. And then she screamed.

An Indian was standing just a few feet from her, watching intently. He was short and very dark skinned, with jet black hair held from his face by a band around his head. He wore long pants, but no shirt. He was handsome and well built, clutching a tomahawk in one hand and a musket in the other.

"Oh no!" she gasped, her hands flying to her mouth.

The Indian walked straight up to her and sniffed at the machine. She leaned away, apprehensively. He ran his eyes over her and then shoved the tomahawk into a strap at his side, reaching out to grip her wrist. He jerked her off the platform and she almost fell as she stumbled to the ground.

"Hey!" she shouted. "Stop that."

She tried to wrench her wrist free but he was far too strong. He jerked hard and she flew past him. He whipped her around in a small circle, shaking his musket, a menacing glare in his dark eyes.

"You come!" he growled.

"No!" she shouted, jerking her wrist free and turning away. "Abe!!!!!!"

The Indian hit her square on the point of her jaw with the butt end of the musket; she sagged, heading for the ground in a slow-motion fall. He scooped her up before she landed and tossed her over his shoulder, glancing wildly about to see if anyone had heard her scream. He heard running and shouting in the forest, and he darted off into the woods, carrying Jenny.

Lincoln and his men burst into the clearing, gasping and looking all around, their muskets at the ready. When they saw the transporter, they stopped dead in their tracks, gawking at it.

"Captain, what the heck is that thing?" said Ezra, walking cautiously around it in a semi crouch.

"More importantly, where is Jenny?" shouted Lincoln, frantically scanning the area. "And why did she scream?"

They spread out, searching for ten minutes but with no luck. Lincoln dropped his musket butt to the soft earth and leaned against the long barrel, sweat dripping off his brow. He wiped it away with a flick of his hand and shook his head, distraught.

"Why did I agree to such a foolish thing," he muttered. "She is my responsibility…and I allow this to happen. I should be shot for dereliction of duty."

They scouted the area for an hour before giving up and trudging dejectedly back to camp.

The body draped over his shoulder was small and light, and Black Hawk moved quickly to the river's edge, where a thin canoe was hidden. Laying Jenny down, he pulled the canoe from its hiding place and then picked her up and laid her down in the canoe. He jumped in, grabbing a paddle and, after a quick glance back over his shoulder, the canoe moved out onto the Rock River. He began paddling furiously for the opposite shore.

Jenny came around slowly, rubbing her face and moving slightly. She sat up halfway and stared at Black Hawk. He saw her movement but said nothing. She watched him for a moment, then lay back down, still groggy from the punch. Minutes later, she was vaguely aware of the canoe striking land. Black Hawk leaped out and grabbed her wrist and half jerked, half lifted her out of the canoe. She faced him on shaky legs.

"Walk," he commanded, pointing in the direction he wanted her to go. She nodded that she understood and started off into the woods. For a brief moment, she thought about taking off and seeing if she could outrun him just like she had the other Indians the night before, but she doubted she could under the best of conditions…and now she felt like her legs were made of lead.

They moved inland quickly, through the dense forest. He didn't touch her again, but she could sense that he was right behind her. She turned halfway once just to make sure and his dark eyes locked on hers. She turned back quickly, determined to not make a fuss, or stumble or fall. She wanted to earn his respect; she wanted to show him that she could keep any pace he forced on her.

Twenty minutes after landing the canoe, they broke into a very small clearing where thirty warriors were standing around a burned-out fire. They had known Black Hawk was coming ever since he arrived on the shoreline, alerting one another through a series of sharp birdcalls.

She stood attentive as Black Hawk described to the others what had transpired, the braves stealing glances at her continually. Except for Black Hawk, they all looked to be young, perhaps anywhere from their late teens to late twenties. All were trim and muscular, and had white stripes painted across their faces. Though she could not understand a word that was being said, she could tell by his body language and by the expressions on the faces of the warriors that Black Hawk was a man of considerable oratorical skills and was a leader of stature.

One of the warriors pointed at Jenny, talking excitedly. Black Hawk turned to stare at her, then walked over to her and gripped her wrist. He pulled her to a small tree and bent down to slide a rope around one foot, tying it securely to the tree. He stood up and faced her.

"He say you run like the wind," said Black Hawk, in passable English. "I must…tie you to tree so that you do not run away."

"You speak English?" she asked, surprised.

"Some," he said. "I learn from Father Dixon, at the village. We were friends, once upon a time. Then too many whites come and they take all our land, not just some land for the village. They make us sign a worthless treaty, so they can force us off our own land."

He returned to the group and they all sat down. He pulled a pouch from his breeches and held it out to the others. He began talking in their tongue once again, so she could not understand a word.

"This is the woman with great magic that we were told by our ancestors would come one day," said Black Hawk.

Several nodded, glancing at her again.

"She came to us," he looked up at the sky, making a great circling motion…"from a sky chariot and can give us great power."

He spilled the contents of the pouch on the ground and sorted through the various rocks and animal teeth; he reached for one perfect bit of rock, a solid light blue stone, and held it up. He stared at it, then handed it to the warrior next to him. The second warrior examined it closely and began to chant, then handed it to the next warrior. It made the rounds and came back to Black Hawk. He stood up and walked back to Jenny.

"Take this, woman," he said, thrusting the bright blue stone toward her.

"Why?" she asked, recoiling from it. "What do you want of me?"

"To carry this totem with you, on your sky carriage," he said.

"My…carriage?" she stammered. "What do you mean?"

"The carriage that still sits in the forest. The carriage that brought you here from the sky," he said.

"The transporter?" she gasped. "Why…in heaven's name?"

"Among our greatest memories is the story of a woman who came from a place far, far away, in the sky. She came, but did not stay. She had great magic; she gave us some of the magic through the blue stone…she gave the stone great power, which we will carry into battle."

"But, honestly, I have no magic," she protested.

Black Hawk straightened up, glaring at her in a very intimidating manner.

"You will give power to the blue stone, for Black Hawk to take into battle. It must be done! We stay here tonight; tomorrow, we go to the carriage. There, you will give magic to the blue stone."

Jenny groaned and pulled the watch from her pocket. Black Hawk watched her closely.

"But, I only have eighty hours to spend, and I have to get to 1932, somehow. I've already been here over fifteen hours."

She spent the rest of the day tied to the tree, but she was able to sit down. She leaned against the tree, watching the Indians converse and plan. Black Hawk glanced at her continually and after awhile he spoke to one of the warriors, who came and offered her water. She drank at great length, not realizing how thirsty she was until tasting the water. Later, she was brought a bowl with berries in it, and some form of meat, which she suspected was venison. She ate ravenously. She leaned against the trunk of the tree, totally exhausted. She watched the band of Indians through eyes that were intent upon closing. She struggled to stay awake and felt a resurgence as the Indians fashioned a small campfire, and sat around it talking into the night.

Black Hawk walked to her at one point, carrying a rolled-up blanket. He stopped and stared down at her; for the first time a trace of a smile ran over his face.

"Here," he said. "It will not get very cold, but still…the warmth of the blanket will feel good as night takes hold."

She took it and smiled weakly.

"Thank you," she whispered. "You are kind."

The smile left his face. He turned abruptly and walked back to the fire, sitting cross-legged with the others. She wrapped the blanket around herself and leaned against the tree. And then sleep overtook her.

Early the next morning, with a heavy dew hanging over the land and the water, the band crossed the river in five canoes. Several stayed with the canoes while Black Hawk and ten warriors moved stealthily through the woods, with Jenny in the middle of the group. They came to the clearing where they could see the transporter. Black Hawk motioned Jenny to be brought up to him.

"The carriage from the sky!" he said, pointing at the machine. "Take the blue stone to it, so it can share in the power."

"Oh, for heaven's sake," she said, exasperated.

Black Hawk gripped her hand and laid the stone in it, and then pushed her out into the clearing. She gaped at him and then shrugged.

"Okay...if that's what you want," she said. She walked briskly toward the transporter and climbed up onto the platform. Black Hawk stayed beside her, but ten yards from the machine he halted abruptly. He was obviously in awe of it. The other warriors had trailed along behind them, cautiously, and stopped when he did. Jenny watched them, smiling at their actions.

"I'm not sure what you're after, but as long as I'm here I might as well make certain I reset this thing correctly," she muttered half aloud. She saw that the dial she had begun tinkering with when Black Hawk found her the previous day had not been firmly set and was back on the same date. She sighed with frustration and pulled out the paper from her pocket again. She spread it on the dial and began studying it anew. Black Hawk moved closer slowly; she pulled out the blue stone and laid it on the dial, too.

"See...here it is," she said. He stopped immediately, mumbling to his warriors.

For several minutes, she read the instructions, then began turning the dials.

"Hmmmm...here...is the problem," she said. "Let's turn this to...June 22, 1932...,"

Suddenly, the machine came alive. She gasped, looking up, startled. The Indians all jumped back at the whirring sound; one of them lifted his bow, placing an arrow on the string, pointing it at the machine. Another jerked his musket up and leveled it at the machine. Everyone was yelling...then the Indian with the musket squeezed the trigger.

A shot rang out. The bullet struck a metal apparatus in front of Jenny and ricocheted off, with a loud, ringing noise.

"No!" Jenny shouted. "Don't shoot the time dial, of all things!"

She stood and shook her fist at the Indian, who tilted his head in bewilderment. Black Hawk lifted his tomahawk and shook it back at her.

Lincoln and six soldiers burst into the clearing on the far side.

"Jenny!" Abe yelled. "Are you all right?"

"Jehosaphat, Abe. It's Black Hawk himself!" shouted Ezra, eyes wide, standing next to Lincoln, his musket raised.

Black Hawk glanced at the soldiers and then swiveled back to face Jenny.

Lincoln and his men stood on one side of the clearing, with Black Hawk and his warriors on the other side. Jenny and the transporter were directly in between them.

"Jenny! What is that...thing?" Lincoln shouted, moving forward.

She threw her hands to her face, framing it, shocked at what she was feeling.

"Abe! The shot activated it. I...I'm...afraid I'm going...," she screamed.

The transporter was whirring and began to quiver. The Indians stared in stupefied amazement, as did the soldiers. Lincoln ran forward, arms outstretched.

"What is happening?" he shouted. "Jenny!"

Jenny grimaced, hands reaching out to Lincoln. She sank into the chair, her legs suddenly very weak.

"Abe, I don't want to go," she yelled. "I don't want to leave you now. Ohhhhh...."

The transporter began to fade from view. Jenny sagged back in her seat and stared hopelessly at Lincoln. He ran to the very front of the platform and tried to reach Jenny, to yank her from it. He received a shock and leaped back. He stared in helpless resignation.

The transporter disappeared. Lincoln and his men stood dumbfounded, looking at one another, then at Black Hawk and his warriors. Black Hawk's eyes had grown wide with disbelief as he watched the drama unfold. He shook his tomahawk at Lincoln, angry at losing both his captive and the blue stone. He turned and ran into the forest, his warriors with him.

Ezra moved next to Lincoln, a stunned expression on his thin features.

"Abe, what in tarnation," he mumbled. "Where...where did she go?"

Lincoln gaped at where the transporter had sat just seconds earlier. He walked over to the spot, running his boots through the long grass. He looked up at Ezra, his thick eyebrows knitted in frustration.

"I don't know, Ezra," he croaked. "I truly don't know."

"She was so dang pretty, Abe. Do you think we'll ever see her again?" Ezra asked.

Lincoln shrugged heavily, his lanky frame sagging.

"Only God knows, Ezra. But...I pray that we will," he said softly.

Chapter Six

The transporter stopped whirring and came to a standstill. Jenny's hands covered her face for several moments after the machine had shut down. She finally looked up and saw the familiar forest landscape. Abe and the Indians were gone. She groaned and slumped in the machine, devastated. She picked the blue stone up from the time dial, rubbing its smooth surface between her fingers, then slipped it into her pocket.

Several minutes passed before she could force herself to step down off the platform and when she did so it was with extreme caution, glancing all about her. She walked a few steps, then went back and picked up her bag. She looked around again and spotted a large log. She plopped down on it and began to cry softly. She sat for a long time, exhausted both mentally and physically. Her legs began to quiver and she dropped both hands on her knees, squeezing them in an effort to regain her composure. Finally, she stopped trembling.

The faint sound of laughter and gleeful shouts caught her attention. Slowly, she lifted her head, listening. She stood and walked cautiously toward the noise. It grew louder and louder. She parted the branches of a tree and stared out at the Rock River. Far in the distance were dozens of boys and girls swimming in a roped-off area of the river. A large slide sat nearby in the water, with swimmers lined up to take the ride down into the water. She gasped and watched for several minutes, enthralled. She saw a park bench off to the side and moved toward it. She sat down, never taking her eyes off the river.

The scene was so tranquil that she momentarily forgot her troubles. She glanced up and down the riverbank and realized she was sitting at the very spot where Lincoln's camp had been...a full century earlier. The thought of Abe and his men standing in front of the transporter made her feel sad again, and she sagged against the back of the bench, her mind jumbled with all that had happened in the last few minutes. Or was it the last few minutes? Had it been in reality one hundred years? Was she locked in some form of a time warp? She could not comprehend all that had happened and how it was happening — or if it was even real. Again, she wondered if the professor was some sort of hypnotist or illusionist and if she was still sitting in her room, back in Iowa City, and only her mind was traveling.

Her thoughts were sharply interrupted by a scream from out in the river. A boy was caught in the current and was bobbing up and down, heading away from shore, in serious danger. She saw his thin arms waving frantically as he screamed again for help. Jenny stood up, terrified. The swimmers were all yelling and gesturing wildly, but no one was doing anything to help the swimmer. She bit her lower lip and edged forward in halting steps. She was a good swimmer...but she did not know if she could save someone.

A figure in a black swimming suit and tank top streaked by, almost running into her. She leaped back, gasping as the young man raced for the water and dove in headfirst. He swam out to the drowning boy with long, powerful strokes and grabbed him under the arms. Then he swam back toward shore, pulling the young boy with him.

The young man in the black suit and black top climbed out of the river, carrying the boy. He laid him gently down on the grass and straddled him, crouching low, his face set in grim determination. He began trying to pump water from the boy's chest. Everyone gathered around, watching the drama unfold.

After several long moments of tense silence, the young boy coughed loudly and spit up some water. He coughed again and his eyes opened. The young man climbed off him and smiled widely, helping the boy to a sitting position.

People in the crowd began chuckling, releasing their pent-up tension. Several clapped.

"Way to go, Ronnie," shouted one of the girls.

"You did it, Dutch," said another. "Billy's going to be okay."

Jenny watched the young lifeguard as he stood up, running a hand through his dark hair, smiling and nodding to those around him. She recognized him from the photo hanging on her wall. It was the Lowell Park lifeguard she had studied for years — standing there in front of her was Ronald "Dutch" Reagan himself.

"Billy, how many times have we warned you about getting out too far?" Dutch said sternly, hands on hips, towering over the young boy. "The Rock has a strong undertow. You know better."

He paused, sensing he was being too rough on the youngster.

"Sometimes I think you want to go off and drown just to get me fired!" he said with a smile.

"Aw, I'm sorry, Dutch," the boy said sheepishly. "I just forgot, and went out too dang far."

Jenny felt weak in her knees and looked back at the bench. She wanted to go collapse on it, but couldn't force herself to leave. She stood at the back of the crowd, listening to the people talk and laugh, her eyes glued on Reagan. She was unaware that another pair of eyes had singled her out and was sizing her up. As the crowd began to break up, heading back to the beach and the water, a young woman strolled up to Jenny.

"Say, are you that Welch girl from over in Sterling?" the girl said, arching an eyebrow.

Jenny stared at the girl, who was a little taller than she was and had long, brown hair and a cute figure.

"Sterling? Why, no. I'm...from Iowa City," said Jenny. "Why do you ask?"

"Are you sure? You look like that Welch girl to me," said the girl, still sizing her up.

"You have me confused with someone else, I'm afraid," said Jenny.

Jenny walked away, the girl staring after her. Jenny trailed behind Reagan, who walked to the edge of the large stone beach house. She recognized it from her drive through the park, when the professor had pointed it out to her. Reagan grabbed a large towel and began to dry off. A number of boys and girls gathered around him, chatting.

Reagan saw Jenny for the first time and nodded politely at her, smiling. He looked away as a little boy tugged at his arm, talking to him. But, several moments later he glanced back over at Jenny. She smiled faintly as their eyes met, and then she turned and walked away, afraid she might faint if she did not get her legs to moving. She walked down to the water's edge, watching the kids on the slide, shouting and splashing. She could hardly imagine the difference in the settings she had undergone. Less than an hour earlier she had been surrounded by wild Indians and Illinois militia led by Abe Lincoln; now, she was watching Dixon kids swimming on a hot summer's day, with Ronald Reagan as their lifeguard.

She was emotionally overwhelmed. She needed to exercise in order to maintain her sanity and to clear away the cobwebs of confusion and doubt. She began to jog down the beach, slowly...

Two hours later, the swimming area was nearly deserted. She sat on the bench and watched as the three lifeguards picked up towels and debris. Reagan was near the water's edge, coaxing some late swimmers out of the water.

"There's always tomorrow. And all summer, for that matter," he told them, motioning for them to come in. "Joe Thompson, you come in now," he shouted to one swimmer out by the slide. Slowly, the stragglers emerged from the water.

With night approaching, Jenny began to worry about where she would go. She dug her hand into her pocket and pulled out the wad of money the professor had given her. From her discussions with the professor, she remembered that the Nachusa House, the biggest hotel, was located in the center of town and had plenty of rooms available.

A voice caused her to turn around.

"Do you have a ride into town?"

It was the same girl who had talked to her earlier. Jenny smiled weakly.

"No, I...I walked out," said Jenny.

"All the way from Dixon? That's almost three miles," said the girl, acting surprised.

"Well, I need the exercise," said Jenny lamely.

"Exercise?" said the girl. "You don't look to me like you need exercise, honey."

Jenny shrugged and stood. She saw Reagan walking toward the stone beach house, talking with the other lifeguards. The girl saw Jenny watching him.

"Are you going to the dance at the high school?" the girl asked.

"Dance? When?" asked Jenny, trying to be polite.

The girl frowned and took Jenny's arm gently.

"Tonight, of course, silly," she said. "It's the annual 'welcome back summer bash,' for all the grads home from college for the summer. It's been advertised for weeks. Everyone's going."

She paused, a sly smile on her lips.

"Dutch will most likely be there…that is, if there isn't a Tom Mix movie playing at the Dixon Theater. He wouldn't miss a Tom Mix or Douglas Fairbanks movie if the school was burning down."

Jenny blushed.

"Oh, that doesn't make any difference, if he's there," she said defensively. Then she looked back at the girl. "But it would just be fun to go."

The girl giggled and looked around to see if anyone was watching them.

"My name is Beverly Grant. I graduated from Dixon High two years ago, and I'm working in town, saving money for college. You don't have to play coy with me. I saw the way you watch his every move. I don't blame you. Lots of girls are in love with Dutch. I used to have a crush on him too, but I've gotten over it. We're just good friends now."

Jenny smiled at Beverly and offered her hand. They shook.

"I'm Jenny Brix. Actually, I'm from Iowa City…just sort of passing through, you know."

"And you wanted to see Dutch?" Beverly asked.

"No. I don't know him at all," said Jenny. "I am interested in…studying," she stopped, not knowing how to proceed. Beverly was staring at her with a half smile.

"Studying…Dutch?" she asked.

"No, no," laughed Jenny.

"Studying what?" asked Beverly. "Do you want to be a lifeguard too?"

"Yes. That's it. I want to be a lifeguard," said Jenny, grateful for an end to the probing.

Beverly seemed content with the answer. She pointed over to a young man headed their way. He was a gangly sort, about six foot, weighing perhaps one hundred and fifty pounds. He had a head of bushy, blonde hair and was adjusting his glasses as he hurried toward them.

"That's Scooter, my best friend. He graduated in 1928, with Dutch, and he's home from college for the summer, too," she said. "If you want to go into Dixon, you can ride in with me and Scooter. His car's not much, but we have plenty of room."

"That would be great," said Jenny.

Soon, they were in a jalopy convertible, motoring down a tree-lined road, on the way from Lowell Park to Dixon. Scooter was driving, with Beverly next to him and Jenny on the outside. Jenny enjoyed the gentle breeze cutting in from the side of the jalopy, brushing her hair back and making her feel relaxed. She leaned back in the seat, gazing out at the countryside. Scooter glanced around Beverly, looking at Jenny.

"So, what are you doing here in Dixon?" he asked, squinting at her for a better view.

"I told you, Scooter, she wants to be a lifeguard," said Beverly. "She's doing research on it."

Scooter frowned, glancing at Beverly.

"And Dixon is the only place in the world you can study life-guards?" he said sarcastically. "She had to come all the way over from Iowa City to do that...like there's no rivers in Iowa?"

"I've heard how pretty Lowell Park is," injected Jenny. "I wanted to visit here. Besides, I needed to get away from Iowa City for awhile, see something new."

"But Dixon is such a boring little place," said Scooter, gripping the wooden steering wheel. "Why would anyone want to come here? Nothing exciting ever happens in Dixon."

"That's not so, Scooter. We have lots to do in Dixon, all the time," said Beverly, punching him softly on the shoulder and glaring at him.

"Yeah? Like what?" he said.

"Well, like the dance tonight," she responded.

"Oh, big deal," he said, one hand flying in the air to show his frustration. "I've had more fun at Sunday school classes."

"Moon Reagan is coming," said Beverly. "He won that Charleston dance contest in Chicago last year. Maybe he'll dance the Charleston. That'll be neat."

"I can hardly wait," said Scooter.

"Oh, you're so cynical. I don't know why I even put up with you," Beverly said, turning toward Jenny, and winking.

"Because I'm so charming," he said.

"Right. A real Rudolph Valentino," giggled Beverly.

"But isn't Valentino dead?" asked Jenny.

Scooter and Beverly glanced at each other, then at Jenny. They giggled as the auto zipped past a sign that said Dixon City Limits. The auto rambled through town, over the bridge which spanned the Rock River, and then zipped up a hill, where it turned right and entered a residential area. They drove past South Central School, an impressive brick structure where the dance was scheduled that night.

"That's the old high school, where Dutch and Scooter graduated from a couple of years ago," said Beverly, making light conversation. "The new high school is on the other side of the river. It's a lot bigger, but I still like this one best. The dance will be here."

Scooter stopped in front of a modest white house in the center of the block. He and Beverly moved out his side of the auto, Beverly motioning for Jenny to join them. She climbed out slowly and stood in front of the auto, looking up and down the street apprehensively.

"C'mon," shouted Beverly to her. "What's wrong?"

Jenny glanced about nervously.

"I hadn't thought all of this through, I guess," she said. "The professor said I should stay at the Nachusa House."

"What professor?" asked Beverly, tilting her head as if trying to understand. Scooter was also watching Jenny very intently.

"Oh, never mind," said Jenny. "I'm just rattling on."

Beverly moved over to Jenny and placed an arm around her shoulder.

"Listen, kiddo, I know you're a long way from home. I'm not sure why, or where you're going, but I do know you need a friend. I could see that right away, back at the park."

She paused to glance at Scooter, who was slouched against the side of the car, arms folded.

"There's not many things I'm good at," she added. "But being a friend is one of them. Right, Scooter?"

Scooter nodded, offering a weak smile.

"Right! For sure!" he said sincerely. "Everyone is Beverly's best friend."

"So, come on. Let's go meet mom, and get ready for the dance," said Beverly, grabbing Jenny's elbow and leading her toward the house.

It was a clean, neat home with a big throw rug covering half of the living room area. A Rudy Vallee song was playing on the wooden victrola. Mrs. Grant was working in the kitchen and walked into the living room when she heard the voices, wiping her hands on her apron. She was a plump woman who looked like an older version of Beverly, with much the same features.

"Well, you're back," she said to her daughter. "Hello to you, Scooter," she added, nodding at him.

"Hi, mom," said Beverly. "This is Jenny. We met her at Lowell Park today. She's going to the dance with us tonight."

Mrs. Grant smiled warmly at her.

"Hello, Jenny…are you a Dixon girl?" she asked.

"No, Mrs. Grant. Actually, I'm from Iowa City, Iowa," she said.

"Are you a student there, at the college?" Mrs. Grant asked.

"Yes," said Jenny. "I was a poli sci major. I'm working on a master's degree now, with an emphasis on presidential studies."

"Oh, that's so interesting," said Mrs. Grant. "I would love to have gone to college. And studying the presidents — my, how fascinating! Washington, Jefferson, Lincoln…such great men."

At the mention of Lincoln, Jenny felt a stab of sadness.

"Yes," she said, wanting to move on quickly and not dwell on Abe. "And FDR; Kennedy, too. They were so charismatic. Of course, my favorite is…,"

She paused, catching herself. The three were staring at her.

"I think it's pretty soon to judge FDR," laughed Mrs. Grant. "He hasn't even won the election yet. It's still Mr. Hoover's job, at least until November rolls around, and then we'll see. But I would guess the nation is going to hold this economic mess against him. And what was that other name you mentioned?"

Scooter and Beverly were watching her closely. Jenny felt very uncomfortable.

"It was just a joke, Mrs. Grant," she said softly. "Please, it was nothing…."

"No matter," Beverly cut in. "I don't want to talk politics anyway. Scooter, you come back and get us at 8 p.m. sharp. And be on time! C'mon up to my room, Jenny. We have to get ready."

There were pictures of movie stars Greta Garbo and Clara Bow on the wall of the bedroom, along with several college pennants.

Beverly fussed in her closet, sorting through various blouses and skirts, muttering the entire time. Jenny sat on the edge of the bed watching her with amusement, and feeling grateful for running into her. She glanced out the window at the setting sun, a strange sense of isolation catching hold of her. She wished she could tell Beverly what she was really doing in Dixon, to share her secret with someone. But knew at this point that no one would, or could, believe her.

Jenny walked to the dresser and glanced at some photos scattered on it as Beverly emerged from the closet, holding out two skirts. She saw a photo of Reagan in his lifeguard suit, the same one she had hanging on her wall in Iowa City.

"This is a nice photo of Ronald Reagan. Where did it come from?" Jenny asked.

"A friend of mine, Bee, took it with her Kodak camera," said Beverly. "Isn't it a hoot? I got it from her last year and just had to put it up."

Jenny continued to stare at it. Beverly came to her side, touching her arm gently.

"Gee, you sure do have a crush on that guy, don't you?" she said.

"No, of course not," said Jenny. "I don't even know him at all. I was just making conversation. But it was pretty impressive what he did today, saving that young boy from drowning."

"Yes, it was," said Beverly with a shrug, holding out the two skirts to check them over again. "He's done that a lot. I know him pretty well, I guess."

"Do you have a thing for lifeguards, Jenny?" she asked, lowering the skirts. "Not that he isn't very handsome. But he's kind of... well, you know."

"No, I don't know," said Jenny. "Tell me, please."

"Well...it's just that he's so...serious," said Beverly. "Almost square. But his brother, Moon, is very different. They used to live just around the corner from us, over on Hennepin Avenue. They've moved since then, though. They live down on Monroe now. Moon's a card. He's real funny, outgoing. A live wire. He's more fun, if you want to know the truth."

"But, Ron doesn't see very well," said Jenny, defensively. "His poor eyesight made him so self conscious as a young boy. Once he got his glasses, he really was able to develop his personality, or so they say."

Beverly laughed, tossing the skirts on the bed, and placing her hands on her hips.

"Say, how do you know so much about Dutch Reagan, for crying out loud. You gotta watch yourself, Jenny; people are going to think you're a little weird if you go around talking about Dutch all the time."

She paused and turned her attention back to the skirts.

"Which one do you like?" she asked. "You pick one... I'll wear the other one."

"Me, in one of those?" laughed Jenny, backing away. "I don't think so."

"Well, you sure can't wear those jeans you've got on now," said Beverly. "Do you have a suitcase hidden somewhere, besides that little bag you're carrying? If not...take your choice.

"You can take your pick of blouses, too, from over there in that dresser. My sister Grace is off to college, in Monmouth. You're about her size. Take any one you want."

Six blocks away, Dutch Reagan lay stretched out on his bed in the tiny bedroom he shared with Moon on the summers they were home from college. This was the fourth house the Reagans had lived in since moving to Dixon when Dutch was just nine years old, and was the smallest. He was still in his lifeguard suit. He had a book in front of him but was not reading it. A small radio sat on the old bureau chest, with a male's voice crackling from it.

"You're awful quiet, little brother," said Moon, sitting in a nearby chair, pulling on his socks and shoes. "Still thinking about that squirt you pulled out of the Rock today?"

"I was earlier, Moon," said Dutch, turning to his back and staring at the ceiling. "But, I really wasn't just now."

Moon stood up, looking down at his shoes. He danced a little jig, turning in a small circle.

"What then? The dance?" he asked.

"Yeah, a little bit," said Dutch. "You know, I always wished I could dance better. Like you, Moon."

Moon looked at his younger brother and smiled faintly. He plopped back down in the chair.

"Aw, c'mon. Stop it," he said. "You never have enough confidence in yourself, Dutch. It's no big deal. You just walk out on the dance floor and your feet will start moving. You dance well enough.

Real good, as a matter of fact."

"Not good enough to win any Charleston contest in Chicago," said Dutch.

"Luck, pure luck...and a darn good partner," said Moon.

"Yeah, a good partner," said Dutch forlornly. "That sure makes a difference in life, doesn't it? Having someone you can trust and count on at your side. Someone to build plans with."

"You still fretting over what's her name?" asked Moon. "Gees, that's ancient history, Dutch. You gotta move on. Forget about her."

"I have," said Dutch, shrugging his shoulders and closing the book. He sat it on the small table and lay back, locking his hands behind his head.

"Oh, then it's someone else, huh?" asked Moon, arching an eyebrow and studying his younger brother. "So...who is it now?"

Dutch didn't respond for several moments.

"How did the Cubbies and the White Sox do today?" he finally asked. "I was trying to get the score on the radio, but I missed it."

Moon walked over and turned off the crackling voice.

"Between the radio and your books, you never do anything exciting," said Moon. "You need to get out and live more, little brother. Now that you've graduated from college, the whole world's your oyster. Just figure out which oyster you're going to crack open and go do it." He stared at Dutch lying on the bed, lost in heavy thought.

"It's not like I thought it would be," Dutch said. "Now that college is behind me, it's still not easy to find a job. This depression we're in is tough on the working man. I didn't think I'd be back as a lifeguard for the seventh straight summer! Not that I mind ...it's a great job. It's just that I'm anxious to get on with real life."

There was a long pause as Moon continued getting ready for the dance.

"So, once again," Moon said. "Do you have a new love interest?"

"Well, no one in particular," Dutch said finally. "But, there was this real pretty girl today, out at the park. I'd never seen her before. She looked different. Real different."

"How different, Dutch?"

Moon made a silly expression and held his hands up to his head, as though he were sporting horns. Dutch chuckled.

"Not *that* different. But there was something exciting about her," he said. "I hope she's at the dance tonight. I saw her leave with Scooter and Beverly Grant."

77

"Then your worries are over," said Moon, spreading out his hands as if the case was made. "Beverly and Scooter wouldn't miss a dance no matter what."

He stood and started to leave, then glanced back at Dutch. "But I hope you're not planning on wearing that stinky old swimsuit," he said. "It may impress the girls at Lowell Park, but it won't smell too good come dance time."

Professor Burns sat on the park bench, looking out over the river, lost in heavy thought. The same jogger he had seen the day before was going by again. He slowed down when he saw the professor and walked over to him.

"Pardon me, but I couldn't help feeling you might need some help," he said, an expression of concern working its way over his face. "Are you okay?"

The professor glanced up at him and waved a hand as if to dismiss any hint of a problem.

"What? Oh, yes, yes," he said. "Just daydreaming, I'm afraid."

The jogger flicked the sweat off his face with his hand.

"Everything is okay?" he asked.

"Of course; but thank you," said the professor.

The jogger nodded and started to move away. The professor began coughing hard. The man stopped and came back, kneeling beside the professor.

"You don't sound well," he said. "Are you alone out here?"

"My...assistant, Brock. He went to take a stroll along the river's edge," said the professor, his eyes watering. He pulled out a hanky and dabbed at his eyes.

"What can I do?" asked the man. "I want to help!"

"Pills. In my coat pocket," said the professor, pointing toward his sports jacket on a nearby park table. The man glanced around; he stood up and hurried to the table, bringing the sports jacket to the professor. The professor nodded his thanks and pulled a small bottle out. He sprinkled two yellow tablets into his hand.

"You'll need some water," said the man.

"In the front seat of the truck," said the professor.

The man sprinted to the truck, found a water bottle, and brought it back. The professor took the pills and swallowed them down with a swig of water.

"I'll be fine in a little while. Thank you, very much," he said, smiling up at the man.

"I'll stay with you for awhile," said the man, sitting down in the grass. "I could use a break anyway. I've run about six miles already."

Chapter Seven

A large group of young men and women had congregated by the brick schoolhouse on the corner lot when Scooter pulled his auto up. A number of other autos lined the streets for several blocks in all directions. Watching the young men and women streaming up the sidewalk and jogging across the street, hollering out greetings to their friends, Jenny felt like she was truly in another time zone, almost as much as when she was with Abe Lincoln and his company of militia a century earlier. All the girls wore long skirts with pleats and white socks, with either loose-fitting blouses or sweaters, even in the summer heat. The young men were decked out in long trousers, mostly of dark colors, and wore shirts neatly tucked in at the waist. Outside the school, on a far corner, a group of college-age men were taking sips from a flask they were passing around.

Dutch and Moon Reagan hit the scene promptly at eight and stood with three other men, watching the new arrivals. One of them waved as he saw Scooter pull up.

"Hey, isn't that Scooter? And Beverly?" said Ralph Devine, a tow-head known for being a straight arrow. "Who's that girl with them? She's new."

"She's new, but she's had an impact on some folks already," said Moon, winking at his brother. Dutch grimaced and kicked him lightly in the shin. Moon jumped, yelping in mock pain.

"Yeah? Well, I can see why. She's a real looker," said Devine.

Scooter, Beverly and Jenny walked up the street, Jenny oblivious to all the stares she was generating. But Beverly was well aware of the impact her new friend was having on the crowd and was pleased about it. She leaned into Jenny, clutching her arm.

"There's Dutch, with Moon and Ralph Devine," she whispered. "I'll introduce you now."

Jenny felt a rush of anxiety and pulled away gently.

"No, can't we wait?" she protested mildly, looking away from Dutch.

"Wait for what? Time's a wasting, honey," said Beverly. "Now is the time."

Jenny tried to protest more, but suddenly they were in front of the three men.

"Hi, guys…have you met Jenny Brix yet?" cooed Beverly, anxious to milk the scene for all it was worth. "She's from Iowa. She's just visiting. She's staying with me."

The three nodded at Jenny, equally ill at ease. Then Moon took over.

"Hey, I'm Moon," he said, flashing a big grin. "This guy is Ralph. This other guy, why I forget his name."

Beverly frowned with false disgust and pushed Moon back.

"Don't pay him any attention, Jenny," she said. Then she turned to Dutch. "Jenny, allow me to introduce Dutch Reagan."

Jenny smiled bashfully at Dutch. He did the same, then extended his hand.

"Glad to meet ya. I saw you at the park today, didn't I?" he said.

Upon hearing his voice, Jenny immediately forgot her anxiety.

"Yes. You were wonderful, pulling that young boy from the river," she gushed. "You saved his life."

Dutch looked down, rubbing his shoe on the grass.

"Well, Billy just swam out a bit too far and...."

"Number sixty-six…and counting!" injected Moon, sauntering back up to the group.

Beverly gaped at him.

"Pardon me?" she said, tilting her head. "What does that mean?"

"Dutch keeps score, you know," said Moon. "On an old log by

the lifeguard house, with notches. Mr. Graybill gave it to him. He puts notches on that log just like a gunfighter from the Old West. That's victim number sixty-six he's pulled out of the Rock, so far."

Dutch looked very embarrassed.

"Shoot, that's just so I can let Mr. Graybill know I'm doing my job," he said defensively. "I don't want him to think I'm not up to it."

Beverly looked suitably impressed. Even Scooter leaned forward, interested.

"Sixty-six people you've saved?" said Beverly, a touch of awe in her voice. "I think that's wonderful, Dutch. Don't you, Scooter?"

"Yeah, really terrific," said Scooter before looking away abruptly.

Dutch was anxious to change the subject, and turned toward Jenny.

"Where did you say you're from...Iowa?" he asked. "Where at in Iowa?"

"Iowa City. I go to the university," she said.

Ralph Devine was suddenly very interested.

"Hey, I go to the University of Illinois. You know — home of the famous Galloping Ghost, Red Grange! Did you ever see the Wheaton Iceman play? He had one big game in Iowa City a couple of years back. Ate up those old Hawkeyes."

"Red...who?" Jenny asked, shaking her head, puzzled.

"What? You don't know who Red Grange is?" Devine asked, placing his hand on his heart like he had been dealt a severe punch to the ribcage. "Why, he's just the greatest football player of all time, is all. They gave him fifty thousand smackers just to sign up with the Chicago Bears pro team."

Moon threw up his hands in protest, shaking his head.

"When you go talking about the best ever, Jim Thorpe wasn't all too bad, Ralph," he said. "Don't forget Thorpe."

Dutch chimed in too.

"How about The Gipper?" he said, throwing his hands up in excitement. "He could do it all...run, pass, kick. He *made* Notre Dame. No one played the game any better than George Gipp."

"Shoot, Dutch, he was a gambler and a drinker," said Devine. "A pool shark, besides. He wasn't near as great as Red Grange or Jim Thorpe, no how."

Moon turned to Jenny.

"Iowa got any football players to boast about?" he said, trying to get her involved in the conversation.

"Gee, I think so. We had Nile Kinnick. He won the Heisman Trophy, I believe. And Chuck Long, too. He was a big star a while back."

The three stared at her blankly.

"The Heisman what?" said Devine, reeling back. "And who are those other guys? I never even heard of 'em. They can't have amounted to much."

"I guess they didn't play until later," mumbled Jenny, looking away. She remembered suddenly from a sports history class she had taken last semester as a fill-in that the Heisman Trophy wasn't created until 1935, and that Kinnick's great senior year, when he won the Heisman, came in 1939. Chuck Long had set numerous passing records and finished second in the Heisman Trophy balloting, to Bo Jackson of Auburn, in 1985. She realized she was going to have to pay more attention to her dates if she didn't want to come off as a real flake.

"Later than what?" asked Moon. The three men looked at one another, then at Beverly and Scooter. Ralph Devine rolled his eyes upward, in exasperation.

"You do know who Jack Dempsey is, don't you?" he said. "The greatest heavyweight champion of all time?"

Jenny paused and then said, "Well, there is this fellow named Muhammad Ali that was pretty good." She stopped cold in her tracks when she saw the expressions on their faces.

"Muhammad...what?" asked Moon. "That sounds like a religious name. Where is that guy from?"

Beverly came to the rescue.

"Enough sports talk. Let's go inside," she said, heading for the door and grabbing Jenny's elbow.

"Jenny, stop acting so strange," she whispered to her, leaning in close as they hurried away. "You're going to scare Dutch away. And everyone else, too, for that matter."

They hustled up the steps and into the building. They moved quickly down the narrow hallways, turning several corners and going up two more flights of steps, until at last they came into the gym on the third floor. It was full of balloons and long streamers hanging from the ceiling. There were high beams in the middle of the ceiling, and a basket on each end, for basketball games during the scholastic season. There were two small sets of bleachers on each side. A bandstand had been erected on the north end of the gym.

The men gathered in one corner and the women in the other. Several couples were dancing to the music offered by a five-man band on the stage, but most were standing around talking. The Reagans moved into the center of a circle of men, talking quietly. Nearly thirty minutes passed before the band began playing livelier music. More couples began dancing. The conversation in the Reagan circle had switched from sports to Jenny.

"Sure, she's pretty, all right. Dang pretty," said Devine, glancing over at Jenny. "But she acts a little batty, if you ask me."

"I don't think so," said Moon. "Heck, she's just…fresh, you know? She seems to be a nice girl."

"Then, how come you ain't danced with her yet, Moon?" said a fourth man.

Moon glanced around at them, and at Dutch in particular.

"Well, maybe I just will. Yep, maybe I just will," he mumbled.

He ambled off to where Jenny was standing with Beverly and several other girls. They all saw Moon coming and turned slightly away, playing coy. All but Jenny; who watched him approach, a look of fascination on her face.

"Care to dance, Jenny from Iowa City?" said Moon, doing a little jig in front of her.

"Well…I…I don't know," she said, startled. She had not counted on being asked to dance with the brother of Ronald Reagan. It was another new wrinkle, like running into Abe Lincoln or being kidnapped by Black Hawk, though certainly not as drastic as the latter. But Moon didn't wait for an answer. He grabbed her hand and headed out onto the floor, performing a little soft-shoe on the way. Jenny giggled and fell in behind him. He turned, slid an arm around her waist and started rocking back and forth, grinning widely at her.

"Say, pretty good," said Moon, starting to shift into high gear as the band began belting out a snappy tune, one that he could really get into.

"I took a class in 1920s dancing in P.E. but I never thought I'd actually use it," Jenny said with a laugh as Moon swung her around.

"Why wouldn't you use it?" asked Moon.

"The 1920s…seemed so remote," she said, dancing hard to keep up with him.

"Shoot. Just a year or two away now," he shouted. "Far as I'm concerned, time is just a matter of perspective, anyway."

They danced around the floor as Beverly, Dutch and the others watched in silent admiration.

"She's pretty darn good," said Beverly, glancing at Dutch. He nodded with a faint smile.

The song ended and Moon and Jenny stood in the center of the floor, catching their breath. He wiped his forehead and then a slower song came on. Without asking, he slid an arm loosely around her waist and they began dancing again.

"You know, my brother thinks you're swell," he said, looking her straight in the eye.

"I think he's swell, too," Jenny said. She tilted her head, smiling at the use of the word she had not heard for years. She realized how grand a word it was. In fact, it was a swell word, she reasoned.

"But, he's kinda shy," said Moon.

"I noticed," she said.

"But, don't hold that against him," said Moon. "He has many good traits. He has a big future ahead of him. He doesn't know it, but I do. He could be manager of the Montgomery Wards store here some day."

Jenny couldn't help but giggle. Moon leaned back, staring at her. He chuckled, too.

"Seriously, he could be running that store some day," said Moon. "I heard him telling mom that just the other day. Why, he might even try to get a job in radio broadcasting. He's talked about that a lot lately, too. Either way, he's got a bright future."

She nodded her head.

"I wouldn't be at all surprised if he did go into radio," she said. "Not at all."

"Say, you really are a bit different," said Moon.

"I...I'm sorry. I..." she began, flustered.

"Don't be sorry," he said quickly. "I meant it as a compliment. You don't find many girls who are as self-assured as you seem to be. It's nice. Real nice."

The song ended and they broke apart. Moon winked at her.

"Thanks for the dance, Jenny from Iowa City," he said. "Maybe Dutch will ask next time."

"I'd like that," she said softly.

But it didn't happen. Dutch stayed away all night long, though she caught him glancing at her several times. He didn't dance with any other girls, either. Though Jenny was asked to dance several times, she declined them all politely. She stayed close to Beverly and Scooter, sipping punch and munching on the cookies that were spread out across a large banquet table.

Close to midnight, an announcement was made that the last dance of the night was coming up. Men walked across the floor to the women, asking for dances. Beverly and Scooter smiled at Jenny as Beverly took Scooter's arm, directing him out onto the floor.

"It took me three hours, but I finally got him to dance this once," said Beverly over her shoulder. Jenny smiled at her, and nodded.

Jenny was asked to dance twice, but she politely refused again. She looked around wistfully, but didn't see Dutch anywhere. She gave a big sigh and walked to the punch bowl. An elderly woman, serving as one of the four chaperones, handed her a glass of punch and smiled sweetly at her. Jenny walked to the far edge of the gymnasium, near a large double door leading out onto a large balcony. She slipped out into the cool night air. She sipped the punch and looked up at the moon overhead. It was hidden behind a layer of clouds so she could scarcely see its outline, but her conversations with the professor about the moon came rushing back to her. She wondered where he might be at that very moment in time. She ran her hands idly over the thin wooden railing in front of her.

A voice behind her caused her to jump.

"Hello. Mind if I join you out here?"

She turned to find Dutch standing behind her. She dropped her glass and it shattered on the floor.

"Gee, I'm sorry if I startled you," he stammered. "I guess I should have been more careful."

"No, that's okay," she said, staring at him and leaning on the railing. She was shocked again to realize what was going on in her life. Staring at the moon, she had almost forgotten where she was. "It's just that…well, two presidents in just one day. I'm…just not up to it."

He bent over and picked up the pieces of glass, dumping them in a nearby receptacle. He walked back to Jenny.

"Two presidents in one day?" he said, a puzzled look on his handsome face. "I'm not sure what you mean, Jenny." He paused. "It is okay if I call you by your first name, isn't it?"

"Yes…sure, of course," she said, flashing a smile.

He smiled too.

"Ralph Devine says you are hiding something, Jenny," he said, straightening up, his brown eyes peering into hers. "Are you?"

Dazzled, she had to shake her head to concentrate.

"Am I...what?" she asked.

"Hiding something?"

She laughed lightly.

"Yes. No. I mean...not really. But then, again...probably," she gaped at him and shrugged helplessly. "So, I guess the answer is... I think I am; but not because I want to. It's just that I have to, at least for now. I guess."

The professor had repeatedly told her that under no circumstances should she reveal where she came from. But she didn't know if that was fair. Dutch stared at her with wide eyes. She felt very foolish and sagged back into the railing.

"This is all so improbable. It can't really be happening," she said so softly that he leaned forward to try and hear what she was saying. "And yet, I think it really is! Abe, Black Hawk...and now you!"

Dutch shook his head, grinning.

"Wow! You really are different."

Jenny sagged even further onto the railing...and it cracked, giving way. She lost her balance and screamed, arms flailing. Dutch leaped to her and grabbed her wrist, jerking her toward him as the railing gave way, and tumbled to the ground behind them, three stories down. She clung to him as they peered over the edge and heard it strike the hard earth.

The doors flew open behind them and people poured onto the balcony, staring at them, then down below. Jenny eased away from Dutch, breathing hard, her eyes locked on his.

"Are you okay?" he whispered. She nodded.

"What the heck was that?" shouted Devine, the first to arrive.

"That old railing finally went," said Dutch. "And Jenny almost went with it!"

Three of the chaperones rushed onto the balcony, pushing past the young men and women. One stretched to look over the edge, then turned to Jenny and Dutch.

"Gracious! Are you both all right?" she asked, hands on her chest.

"Yes! Ron...he saved me," croaked Jenny, nodding at Dutch.

"Chalk up number sixty-seven. But make a notation — this one out of water!" said Moon, slapping his brother gently on the shoulder.

Everyone laughed and began to file back inside to the dance floor. Two older men, school administrators, rushed onto the balcony, looking over the edge and talking quietly as a janitor began picking up pieces of the railing on the ground. The administrators asked Jenny if she was all right, and then requested that they all go back inside. After they filed inside one of the administrators locked the balcony doors.

"Scooter and I are going for a ride," said Beverly after several minutes. "Maybe get a malted." She glanced at Jenny, then at Dutch. They were staring at each other.

"So...would you two like to come along?" Beverly asked.

"Yoo hoo! You two!" she said, getting no response. "I'm speaking to you."

Dutch turned to Beverly, embarrassed.

"I'm sorry, Beverly," he said meekly. "What did you say?"

Beverly feigned exasperation.

"I said...we're going for a malted. Would you two like to join us?"

"Sure!" Dutch said. "That is, if Jenny doesn't mind."

Jenny didn't say anything, standing motionless and looking at Dutch, still obviously a bit shaken by what had just happened on the balcony. Beverly stepped forward and grabbed Jenny's wrist and jerked her along behind her.

"I think I can speak for Jenny," she said. "She definitely doesn't mind!"

They drove to the ice cream shop on Main Street. Though the building was dark, they clamored out of the auto. They peered inside, faces up against the glass.

"Gash darn! I forgot. It closes at midnight," said Scooter.

"You'd think Mr. Hey would stay open later on dance nights," said Beverly. "He's sure missing lots of business. If I ever own my own malt shop, I'm staying open until 3 or 4 in the morning."

"Do you want to own a malt shop, Beverly?" asked Jenny.

"She'd like to, but there's no money in it," said Scooter. "Selling hamburgers and malteds isn't going to get a person anywhere in life."

"She could franchise them out," said Jenny. "That's the way to go. There is a fortune to be made then. Look at McDonald's, and...."

"What do you mean, franchise out?" said Scooter.

"It's a term that means selling your concept of business to other people," said Jenny. "They pay you for the expertise that you have learned and developed. It works very well and has become one of the cornerstones of American free enterprise."

She stopped short again, seeing the other three watching her with perplexed expressions.

"How come you know so much about business and enterprise?" asked Scooter. "Girls aren't supposed to know that kind of stuff."

"Says who?" said Beverly, hands on hips, frowning at Scooter.

"C'mon, Beverly," he said defensively. "You know you don't know anything about business matters. No girl in Dixon does."

"Is that so? Dutch, you don't agree with Scooter, do you?" she asked, turning to him. "You don't think all girls are stupid when it comes to real matters, do you?"

Dutch threw up his hands, grinning sheepishly while backing away.

"Now, don't drag me into this Beverly," he said. "I don't want to get caught between you and Scooter in any argument."

She shook her head in frustration, walking away.

"Ronald Reagan, diplomat!" she muttered. They all laughed as they headed for the auto.

Scooter pulled out his watch, and shook his head.

"Geez, it's getting late, Beverly," he said. "I better take you home. I got a busy day tomorrow. Dutch, ya want a lift home?"

"Sure, thanks," he said.

Just five minutes later, Scooter pulled up in front of a two-story, somewhat battered looking white house, with an old porch. Dutch climbed out of the car, leaning against the auto.

"Sorry I couldn't get you that malted, Jenny," he said. "Maybe tomorrow night?"

"I'd like that. Very much," she said. She leaned out the widow and watched him as he walked slowly up the yard to the porch. She could see a small light inside the house, and saw him watching their auto as it moved away down the street. She finally leaned back in her seat, looking up at the big moon overhead.

"You're home," Scooter mumbled a couple of minutes later as he stopped the car in front of the Grant house. "Gads, I'm tired. I can't wait to get into bed."

After Scooter pulled away, Beverly and Jenny tiptoed along the porch and slipped quietly into her house. As they started up the stairs, Beverly put a finger to her lips.

"Shhhhhh! We don't want to wake mom," she whispered.

Safely in her room, she turned on the light on her dresser, and gave out with a big sigh, plopping down on the bed.

"That Scooter! He's a pip sometimes," she said.

"You really like him, don't you?" said Jenny.

"Sure. He's nice," said Beverly. "But there's another reason. He's very smart. He's got a good head on his shoulders, my dad says."

She paused, then turned over on her stomach, hands beneath her chin, and smiled at Jenny.

"But how about you, and Dutch?"

"Me and Dutch?" asked Jenny. "What about us?"

"Well for starters, he asked you out for tomorrow, a date already! Dutch doesn't usually move that fast when it comes to girls. He's awful darn fast when it comes to diving in the river to save someone's life, but when it comes to girls — that's another matter all together!"

"A date? No, not really. He just asked if I wanted a malted," protested Jenny.

"Honey, I don't know if you're from this decade or what…but where I come from, that's a date, pure and simple!" said Beverly.

Jenny sank onto the second bed.

"Are you sure your mother won't care if I stay the night?" she asked pensively.

"Jenny, she won't care if you stay the month," said Beverly. "That's just the way things are at our house. Forget that; don't worry."

Jenny smiled at her, relieved and thankful for finding someone like Beverly. She was a very sweet person and a wonderful friend for someone who was a long way from home; in fact, almost sixty years from home!

"Thank you, Beverly. I'm lucky I met you," she said. She yawned and stretched out on the bed. "I'm actually still a little shook up from the railing giving way at the dance. And I'm very tired. The professor warned me that I'd be soooo tired. Time travel does that."

She closed her eyes. Beverly watched her, then laid her head down too, exhausted. Soon, they were both sound asleep. Beverly had a dream about Scooter and the dance that night. Jenny dreamed first about a young militia leader from 1832, and then about a dashing lifeguard from 1932….

The professor and Brock sat on the bench by the river watching a family of ducks splashing in the water. Off in the distance, they saw a pontoon boat drift slowly past, with several people on the deck. They waved at the two men on shore, and the professor waved back.

"Do you think she's watching the time close enough?" asked Brock finally, leaning back against the bench, his big arms folded across his thick chest.

The professor winced.

"She knows she has just eighty hours to spend on one trip," he said. "I repeated that over and over. I'm sure she's keeping track."

"She better be," said Brock, pulling out a small note pad from his pocket. "She had seven hours there the first day, arriving at 5 p.m. Then two twenty-four hour days in back to back days, for a total of fifty-five hours last midnight. It's now noon...so she has sixty-seven hours down, with just thirteen left to go before she has to come back."

They stopped talking as they saw the jogger approaching. He waved and ran over to them, halting a few feet away and walking the rest of the way, sporting a wide smile.

"Glad to see you looking so good, professor," he said.

"I feel much better," he said. "You left yesterday before Brock got back. I want you to meet him."

The professor introduced them, Brock being his usual reserved self.

"Glad to meet you, Brock," said the jogger. "My name's Brad Taylor. I jog through the park almost daily. Don't get to see many folks in this part of the park, actually."

Brock scarcely nodded. He wasn't much for small conversation with people he didn't know.

"Are you still waiting for your traveling friend?" Taylor asked the professor.

"Yes. No word yet," said the professor.

"Well, I'd better get going, don't want to lose a good sweat," said Taylor. He moved off down the path and soon was gone from sight. Brock watched him until he disappeared.

"There's something about him that I don't like," said Brock.

"Brock, you're a suspicious man by nature," said the professor, chuckling.

"Yeah; well, there's something about him, nonetheless," he said. "How did he know you are waiting for a traveler?"

"I told him after he helped me with the pills," said the professor. "He wanted to stay around until he knew I was all right. I merely said we were waiting here for a traveler, and weren't sure what day she was coming...but that we had nothing better to do than wait, anyway."

Brock fingered his short beard, squinting down the road.

"And he believed that?"

The professor turned to glance at Brock.

"Of course. Why shouldn't he?"

Brock had nothing more to add to the conversation.

Chapter Eight

It was a bright, beautiful morning as Beverly and Jenny drove into Lowell Park, passing the little park house at the entrance. They drove past the large open area, sheltered by the big trees all around, where boys liked to play football and then proceeded onto the road that offered the spectacular view as it spiraled down to the basin area, and the beach.

"It was nice of Scooter to let us have his car today," said Jenny, glancing a bit nervously at Beverly as she gripped the steering wheel hard. She paused and then offered, "You don't really drive much, do you, Bev?"

Beverly was staring straight ahead, concentrating on the winding road. She had slowed the car to about ten miles an hour as they began the descent, forest all around them.

"No, not a lot. We only have one car and dad needs it for work all the time," said Beverly, biting her lower lip nervously.

"Why didn't Scooter come with us, anyway?" asked Jenny, trying to take her mind off the fact that one small slip by Beverly could send them hurdling over the edge. It was a hard, straight drop-off in many places, with no guard rails at all.

"He said he was going to the library to do some research," said Beverly. "But I think he gets tired of coming to the beach and seeing all the girls making a fuss over Dutch and the other lifeguards."

They made it to the bottom with no problems and both sighed a bit as the auto moved into the open stretch at the basin. They saw Dutch and two other lifeguards standing on the dock that connected to the slide, watching swimmers move into the river. There was a large crowd of happy, shouting swimmers of all ages. Several were standing on a large red object called a spinner. It was anchored to the bottom of the river and spun like a top as kids climbed onto it, trying to grip the large circular handle in the center.

When Dutch spotted Jenny and Beverly, he walked briskly over to their auto.

"Hello, ladies. Beautiful day, isn't it?" he said, flashing his big grin.

Beverly turned to Jenny with a sly smile.

"He calls us ladies, even!" she said. "He must be up to something."

"Hi...Ron," said Jenny. She had awoken with a start just an hour or so earlier, after her fitful sleep, afraid that it was all just a dream. She had turned quickly to make sure Beverly was there and when she saw the empty bed a panic seized her. Then Beverly came strolling in, brushing her teeth, chattering away, and Jenny knew she would see Dutch at least one more time. She was now in the third day of her trip, with time slipping away.

"I'm due for a break," said Dutch, staring at Jenny. "Can I get you two a hot dog?"

"I'm famished," admitted Jenny.

"I ate before Jenny woke up," said Beverly. "She was so anxious to come out here that I couldn't get her to eat anything. You two run along and get your hot dogs. I want to see someone."

Beverly departed, casting a glance back over her shoulder. She winked at Jenny.

"She sure is nice," said Dutch, watching her walk away.

"She's been wonderful to me. And Scooter has been, too," said Jenny. "It seems like I've known them for years...not just...oh my goodness...not just one day!"

"Scooter, he's a bit different," said Dutch. "A nice guy, but with some weird ideas. Some times, I don't know what he's talking about."

They strolled to the hot dog stand and Dutch ordered two sandwiches and sodas. He dug into his shorts to pull out some money but turned the pocket inside out. He looked at Jenny with a pained expression.

"Flat busted! Broke! I can't believe it!" he gasped.

He turned to the man in the hot dog booth, who was leaning on the counter with a bemused expression.

"Dutch...you broke again?" asked Mr. Hey, the same man who owned the malt shop downtown. "What do you do with all that money Mr. Graybill pays you, anyway?"

"Gosh, I'm sorry, Mr. Hey," Dutch said. "I forgot my money at home. Can I pay you tomorrow?"

Before Mr. Hey could answer, Jenny pulled out a dollar bill and placed it on the counter.

"No, Jenny! This is supposed to be my treat," moaned Dutch.

"That's okay," she said. "You can treat me to malteds tonight."

Mr. Hey gave her back two dimes, and they walked away with their hot dogs and drinks.

"Thanks...but, it's not right," said Dutch. "A girl shouldn't have to pay."

Jenny laughed.

"Don't worry," she said. "It's called women's lib. Some day, it will be accepted everywhere."

He shot her a perplexed look as they walked leisurely down the bank of the river, away from the swimming area. They came to a grassy area and Jenny sat down, looking up at Dutch as she took a bite of her hot dog. Dutch plopped down on a nearby log, looking out over the river. They finished off their hot dogs and sodas quickly.

"That was great. But I still shouldn't have let you pay, Jenny," he said.

"Look at it this way," she said, squinting into the bright sun behind him. "It's an investment. Now, I have to make sure you take me out for a malted tonight, just so I can get even."

He smiled warmly at her.

"You sure are something, Jenny from Iowa," he said. "Tell me, how long are you going to be in Dixon, Jenny?"

The question caught her off guard. She moved to the thick grass next to him and sat down in it. She gazed out across the river.

"Not...much longer, I'm afraid," she said. "I can only stay another day, or less. In fact, I may even leave late tonight."

He was surprised and not a little disappointed.

"But, you can come back, right? Iowa City's not that far away."

Jenny frowned, feeling a bit nauseous.

"Iowa City isn't far, true. But it's…a bit more complicated than just driving there, Ron."

Now he was beginning to look very concerned.

"Complicated?" he asked, turning to face her directly. "In what way?"

"It's really hard to explain," she said, fidgeting. She uttered a huge sigh, and glanced up at the sky, then turned back to him. "But, I don't want to talk about that now. Can we just walk some more?"

"Sure," he said, scrambling up off the log and reaching to help her up from the grass. They walked along the riverbank again, in silence. Without realizing it, she pulled the blue stone from her pocket and fiddled with it.

"That stone is neat; when did you get it?" he said, staring down at it.

"Yesterday," she said.

"From around here?" he asked.

"Right across the river, actually," she said, gazing over at the opposite shore. She handed it to him and he turned it over several times, inspecting it.

"It's really unique," he said. "I've never seen anything quite like it before. So smooth…and such an unusual shade of blue."

"It was given to me by someone…special," she said. She paused and then looked at him.

"Ron, do you have any heroes?"

"Sure," he said. "Tom Mix; he's my favorite movie star. I like William S. Hart, too. As far as books go, I love to read Edgar Rice Burroughs books. Horatio Alger and Jack Armstrong stories, too. Actually, I like almost any kind of book."

"I know you love to read," said Jenny. "Or…I mean, I would guess you love to read, from what you just said."

He missed her reference to knowing something about him that she shouldn't. Instead, he launched off on a small discourse about the joy of books.

"Truth is, I've loved to read ever since I was old enough to know what a book is," he continued cheerily. "Both Moon and I spent a lot of time at the city library when we were growing up, mom saw to that. She made sure we were aware of the power of books at an early age. But I think I was there more often than Moon. The great thing about books is that they can take you away to any place you want to go.

"And, they are good companions," he said, glancing back at

her. "No one can be lonely who has a book for company."

Jenny giggled at that statement.

"Sort of like a dog, then?" she asked. "A book can be like a dog…man's best friend?"

"Sure, why not?" he replied, grinning widely, bouncing the blue stone in his hand.

"Well, actually, I meant real life people as heroes, not fictional characters," she said gently.

He rubbed his chin, thinking hard.

"Well, gee; George Gipp, the Gipper, of Notre Dame is one. What a great football player, and he had a very sad ending to his life. He was only about twenty-six years old when he died. I wish they'd make a movie about his life story. I would love to see that. I'd probably sit through it a dozen times, if they had the right actor playing him." He paused, reflecting, then continued.

"And Lindbergh. Who doesn't admire Charles Lindbergh, flying the Atlantic Ocean all alone? Gosh, that was incredible. My dad talked about it for weeks. There's nothing my dad admires more than individual gumption — a man who gets up in the morning and sets about his task, not afraid of hard work or a big hurdle in front of him. 'Go to it,' my dad always says. And that's what Lindbergh did, for sure."

"Oh, they did make a movie about Lindbergh," she offered brightly. "It's one of my favorites. It starred Jimmy Stewart."

"You're kidding, right?" he said. "I woulda known if there was a movie about Lindy. And I've never heard of Jimmy Stewart."

She shook her head again, disappointed in herself for forgetting.

"Uhhh, yes, I was kidding," she said. "Anyone else you admire a lot?"

"Being a swimmer myself, I kinda admire Johnny Weissmuller," he said. "Think of it…all of those world records and gold medals in the Olympics. He's a Chicago fella, you know, and learned to swim in Lake Michigan. Now he's out in Hollywood, making a new Tarzan movie. I heard that on the radio just the other day."

"Do you listen to the radio a lot?" she asked.

"All the time, especially station WLS in Chicago," he said. "Moon says I listen lots more than I should but I really enjoy it. I've even toyed with the idea of trying to become a radio announcer. I think it could be an exciting career, one that's going to grow in the years ahead. I believe radio has a big future in this country, don't you?"

She nodded, enjoying hearing his thoughts, determined to keep probing.

"How about presidents? Who do you like the most among presidents?"

"Why, Lincoln, of course," he said. "Did you know he camped right here in Lowell Park, during the Black Hawk War? He was a captain in the Illinois militia, just twenty-two or twenty-three years old at the time. Just think, one hundred years ago he could have been standing right here, where we are now, saying something profound. Isn't that something?"

The thought nearly took her breath away. She walked along the shore, slowly, Dutch trailing along behind her, still holding the blue stone. She stopped and peered across the river, to where Black Hawk's camp was.

Dutch handed her the stone and she slid it back into her pocket.

"I wonder what he was really like, old Honest Abe," he thought aloud.

"A wonderful person, very warm and caring," she croaked. "I... miss him, a great deal."

"Miss him? I don't follow you, Jenny," he said, shaking his head slowly.

"No, of course not, Ron," she said. "I apologize. I meant, I miss knowing him. I would have liked to have known him, if only for a day...."

"That's a swell idea. Knowing great men, like presidents, even if only for a day," he said, enthused. "I wonder what kind of an impact that would have on your life."

Jenny stared at him strangely, as though she was fearful he knew her secret. He smiled at her, picked up a stone, and tossed it out over the river. It skipped across the water, bouncing several times.

"Can I tell you a secret?" he said. "Sometimes, when I'm real tired and it's been a long day, I throw a rock, just like that. I make it skip. When the kids look up and ask what it was, I say, 'Oh, nothing, probably just a big, old water rat.' Then, they clear out fast. Swimming is over for the day and I get to go on home, a bit early for once."

Jenny started giggling, and then laughed loudly. She leaned against a tree, her body shaking with laughter. Ron laughed too and placed his hand on the tree by her, leaning against it. They continued chuckling, then stopped abruptly. They stared at one another, until Jenny pushed away from the tree.

"This park is so beautiful, Ron," she said, her voice soft. "I just love it out here. Don't you?"

"Yeah, the beauty and the history," he said. "Back in Abe's day, there were Indians all around here. At night, it was plenty scary, what with Black Hawk on the prowl and all."

They continued walking down the shoreline, Dutch tossing a rock every now and then into the water. He talked about his job as a lifeguard, telling her that it paid fifteen dollars a week and was a seven-day a week job, from mid morning until dark. It was a job that he obviously enjoyed a great deal. And he took the lifesaving part very seriously.

"There were some drownings out here in years past, and there was serious talk about closing the beach part down," he said. "Ed and Ruth Graybill are in charge of the park concessions and I applied to them to be a lifeguard. They knew I was a good swimmer from all my time at the YMCA. So...they gave me the job, along with a couple of other fellows. And we haven't had any drownings since, glad to say."

She felt the pride in his voice and the sense of satisfaction he felt from helping others. He nodded at her, his jaw set tight, as if saying..."There! Now you know all about me!" She couldn't help smiling at him.

He sighed and his demeanor changed. He was ready to be less serious.

"But there are lots of good benefits to being a lifeguard," he said. "You get plenty of exercise and get to be outdoors all day long. And, of course, a good tan.

"Being a lifeguard also provides a good opportunity to learn about people," he said. "I like to watch people, observe how they react to various situations. Most don't like being helped all that much. Not many ever thank me for pulling them out of the water. Guess they are a bit embarrassed by it all. Except Billy yesterday."

"Doesn't anyone ever thank you?" she asked surprised. "I would think they would be very appreciative of your efforts. I would think they would even offer some money for being saved."

He shook his head, grinning with a recollection.

"The only money I ever got was from an elderly fellow who lost his upper plate while going down the slide," he said. "I dived and dived for it...and just got lucky. I came up with it, and he was so happy he gave me ten dollars."

They both laughed. They found a park bench and sat down, staring out over the Rock.

"How did you happen to pick Eureka College?" she asked. "I've never really heard of it before you...went there. It's a very small school, isn't it?"

"Yeah, about two hundred and fifty students is all," he said. "But gee, it's beautiful there. It's about twenty miles from Peoria. I've wanted to go there ever since Garland Waggoner enrolled. He was four years ahead of me and a terrific football player at Dixon High. He was captain of the Eureka football team, too. I decided to go to Eureka to follow in his footsteps."

"Did you have a scholarship to play football?" she asked. She was anxious to know more about his college days and how he managed to pay for his education, realizing he did not come from a family of means. She had read several times that paying for college was a real struggle for him, and that the money he managed to save from his lifeguard job at Lowell Park was essential.

"Only a little tiny one, which covered about half of my tuition," he said. "I played football and was also on the swimming team. But I had a job that helped pay my board and keep. I washed dishes in a frat house for the first two years, and then cleaned tables in a girls' dorm for awhile. Last year, I got a job working in the college pool as a lifeguard. I also helped coach the swimming team last year."

She was enjoying listening to him tell her about his college days. She studied his face as he talked, noticing how expressive he had become and how much he was beginning to open up around her.

"You were involved with a drama course, weren't you?" she asked.

He nodded, eager to keep talking. He leaned forward, hands on his knees.

"Oh, the world of drama," he said with a deep voice, slipping into a role. "Yes, my dear." Then he laughed, and his shoulders slumped, somewhat embarrassed. "I guess I got the acting bug a little bit in high school. Dixon has a wonderful drama coach, named B. J. Fraser. He's a terrific teacher, with a great sense of humor. In my junior year, I played the role of Ricky in the Philip Barry play, You and I. Then, my senior year, I was a villain in the George Bernard Shaw play, Captain Applejack.

" I loved doing it," he said. "I guess at heart I'm sort of a ham."

102

There was a long silence. Abruptly, Jenny turned to face him. "You're going to miss college now that it's over, aren't you?" she asked.

"Sure," he said. "I liked the involvement. I know kids who go to school and never participate in anything. I just can't understand that. You learn as much from all the extracurricular opportunities in high school and college as you do from going to classes. I wouldn't trade my degree from Eureka College for a degree from the biggest university in the land.

"One of my favorite sayings is you get out of life what you put into it, and I believe it holds true in school as much as anywhere in life."

She decided to take a drastic change in the direction of their talk. She simply had to ask him one certain question.

"If you could go anywhere back in time — anywhere at all — where would you go?" she asked, her eyes sparkling with excitement.

"Gee, I don't know," he said, surprised at the turn in the conversation. "That's a strange question. I never gave it any thought before."

"Please. For me..." she said, taking his hand in hers. He swallowed heavily.

"Let's see, then. The Revolutionary War period, I guess. To see George Washington."

"Not Lincoln?" she asked, disappointed.

"Sure, Abe, too," he said. "Unless I'm limited to just one pick."

She was very excited, squeezing his hand.

"What would you ask him?"

"Who?" he asked, smiling at her. He was enjoying the game now, too. "George or Abe?"

"Either one; no — Abe. What would you ask Abe Lincoln, if you could ask him anything at all?"

"Hmmmmm. Let's see...I'd ask him if...he ever knew a girl as sweet as Jenny from Iowa," he said.

She pulled her hands away, as if she might pout.

"Ron, I'm serious," she said. He looked into her brown eyes, moving closer. She gazed up at his tanned face and shoulders, and the strand of black hair that had fallen across his face. He was incredibly handsome at that moment, like a young movie star.

"Well, so am I, Jenny," he said. "I really like you. I...I've never known anyone as stimulating as you are. Or as interesting. It's like there is this great mystery surrounding you."

She leaned into him and her hands found his right hand again, closing on it.

"I'm not really all that mysterious," she whispered. "I'm really quite simple. It's just that I'm from...from...."

He was moving slowly toward her, about ready to embrace her, and kiss her.

"Yes?" he mumbled.

"From a different time," she said finally.

He leaned back from her, his hands still in hers.

"Gee, what do you mean?"

She bit her lower lip, staring up at him. She wasn't sure how to proceed, what else to say. She wanted very much to confide in him, but remembered the professor had warned her against telling anyone about her real origins, less they think she was mad.

"Don't you have to get back to work?" she blurted out.

He gasped.

"Holy cow! Yes, you're right," he said, startled. "I was only going to take a ten-minute break. That was about an hour ago."

He started to run away, then turned and ran back to her.

"Malteds tonight?" he asked. "I'll come by Beverly's at about eight, if that's okay."

"Sure!" she said.

He was off and racing down the beach, and shouted over his shoulder at her.

"Don't forget, Jenny."

She watched him dash down the bank, toward the swimming area far off, her heart pounding. There was a quality about him that she had never seen in anyone else, a sense of sincerity that was very charming and drew her to him. She moved to the water's edge, gazing out across the river, where just two days earlier she had been in Black Hawk's camp. She removed her special watch and looked down at it, her mind spinning with confusing thoughts and ideas. Maybe, just maybe, she would miss the deadline, and stay in 1932.

Back at Beverly's house, she and Beverly sat on the back porch swing as it swayed gently. Bev's mother brought them some lemonade and they all three sat on the porch chatting.

"You girls look tired," said Mrs. Grant. "You know, being out in the hot sun all day can exhaust you. Make sure you drink plenty of lemonade. A body needs fluids on a steamer like today."

"Thanks, Mrs. Grant," said Jenny. She drank the glass nearly empty and poured some more from the pitcher on the table.

"So, how do you like Dixon, so far, Jenny?" asked Mrs. Grant.

"I love it. Everyone is so nice and friendly," said Jenny. "And Lowell Park is the most beautiful place I have ever seen. Do you know how it got its name?"

"It was a gift of the James Lowell family, to the city of Dixon," said Mrs. Grant. "He was a rich man who lived out east and bought land here to live on some day. But he was killed in the Civil War. His widow eventually donated the land to the city of Dixon. And did you know John Deere lived near here, too? He built his famous plow at a little spot called Grand Detour, just three miles up river from Dixon."

Beverly grimaced.

"Mom's a real history buff, as you can tell," she said.

"Yes. And proud of it," said Mrs. Grant. "We've even had some presidents stay here in Dixon, at various times."

"Who…besides Abe Lincoln?" Jenny asked, leaning forward, eager to learn more.

"Zachary Taylor was an officer here during the Black Hawk War," said Mrs. Grant. "And so was Jefferson Davis, who became the only president of the Confederacy. And let's see, who else… oh yes…Ulysses S. Grant stayed at the Nachusa House, up in the center of town, after he served as president."

Jenny nodded, impressed with both the list and with Mrs. Grant's knowledge.

"Maybe some day Dixon will produce a president of its very own!" she offered.

"Now, wouldn't that be something," said Mrs. Grant.

Beverly chimed in, too.

"It will probably be Scooter," she said. They all three chuckled.

"But I bet Jenny thinks it would be Dutch Reagan," she continued.

Anxious to change the subject, Jenny turned to Mrs. Grant again.

"What are the Reagans like, Mrs. Grant. Do you know Dutch's mom at all?"

"I know that family well. Mrs. Reagan — Nelle, to her friends — is near to a saint, one of the finest women God ever made," she

105

said. "When the family moved in from Galesburg, or was it Tampico, she made more friends faster than any person I've ever known. She's a member of several clubs and very active in her church. Why, she even boards former prisoners at the house from time to time, helping them find the strength to straighten out their lives."

"I hear Mr. Reagan has…well, a drinking problem," said Jenny gingerly.

"Oh, posh!" she said, waving her hand as if to dismiss the charge. "He's an Irishman, and what Irishman doesn't like to have a beer or two now and then? That rumor has been around for years; but from what I can see, Mr. Reagan's a good provider. He's moved a bit in his earlier days, but the family seems to have found roots now. The Reagans are good folk. I say you can judge the parents by what the kids turn out to be. We'll just have to wait and see if Moon and Dutch amount to a hill of beans some day. My guess is that they will do just fine."

They heard the sound of a car screeching out in front.

"It sounds like Scooter," said Mrs. Grant with a sigh of resignation. "Lord, I wish that boy would learn to drive…sensibly, I mean."

She stood and left the girls on the porch just as Scooter came tearing around the side of the house.

"Beverly, I need to talk to you, right away," he gasped. "In private!"

"Oh, Scooter. Anything you have to say, you can say in front of Jenny," she said.

"Not this," he said emphatically.

"Well, I'm not moving. I'm too tired and too hot," said Beverly.

Jenny stood up and walked down the steps.

"That's okay, Bev. I want to take a walk around the neighborhood, anyway. Maybe I'll go by the Reagan house," she said.

"This will just take a minute," Scooter said apologetically as Jenny eased past him.

Scooter watched Jenny walk across the yard and out of sight. He dashed up the steps and sat down next to Beverly. He had a very anxious look in his eyes.

"Those hot dogs Dutch and Jenny ate today at the beach?" he began.

She glanced at him, bored and a little frustrated at his antics.

"What about them?" she asked.

"Jenny paid for them," he continued.

106

"Oh, Scooter. So what?" she said. "Dutch spent all his savings on college. And he probably didn't have any money with him out at the beach, anyway."

Scooter swallowed heavily, gaping at her.

"She paid for them...with fake money!"

Beverly sat up straight, glaring at him.

"What did you say? What do you mean...fake money?"

"Mr. Hey owns the hot dog stand. He noticed the bill looked different. He got to checking it out. Heck, Bev, it wasn't even printed until 1985. At least, that's what the series date is on the bill itself! There's no doubt that it was fake money."

She sank back in the chair, pondering what it all meant.

"I'm...I'm sure there is a logical explanation," she said finally.

"I hope so, Bev," he said. "I really do. She's a sweet kid, but she seems real mixed up. Like she doesn't really know where she is. I hope she's not some kind of con artist. I've read about people like that who come into a small town and...."

Beverly interrupted him in mid-sentence.

"Last night, before she fell to sleep, she said something very strange."

"Yeah? What was that?" he asked, leaning forward, eyes narrowing.

"She said...something like time travel really tires her out," said Beverly. "That a professor told her that was so. I thought she was so tired that she was just dreaming out loud."

As they sat silently on the porch, eyeing each other, Jenny turned the corner and saw the Reagan home. She stopped in front of it, facing the small porch. A thin woman in her early fifties was sweeping it off. Jenny decided to approach her and took a deep breath.

"Hello, Mrs. Reagan," she said, walking slowly up the sidewalk. Nelle Reagan looked up, stopped sweeping and smiled widely.

"Hello, there. How are you?" she asked sweetly, resting on her broom handle. She wore a long, plain dress, with black shoes. Her auburn hair, streaked with gray, was pulled back in a tight bun. She was not a pretty woman, but she had an engaging smile, one that made people feel immediately comfortable with her.

"Actually, I'm wonderful, Mrs. Reagan. Just wonderful. I just wanted to stop by and say hello, even though you don't know me," she said.

"That's very sweet, child," she said. "Please, come up and sit a spell. It's so hot, and I need a rest."

Jenny walked up the steps and sat on a wooden chair on the porch. Mrs. Reagan settled onto the porch swing.

"I guess we haven't met before," said Mrs. Reagan, looking closely at Jenny. "I thought I knew most of the girls in town who are the same age as Moon and Dutch. Do you know the boys?"

"Oh, yes, I do. They are wonderful boys, both of them," said Jenny.

"A mite mischievous, sometimes," chuckled Mrs. Reagan. "Especially Moon, I'm afraid. But good at heart. They care about others. That's what I'm most proud of."

"They're going to do good works in life, Mrs. Reagan," said Jenny. "I know that." She paused, then continued. "Particularly Dutch. He's going to…make you very, very proud of him, some day."

"How nice of you to say, dear," said Mrs. Reagan. "And my, you seem so sure of it!" She took a long look at Jenny. "You wouldn't be that new girl, from Iowa, by any chance?"

Jenny blushed a bit.

"Why…yes, yes I am," she said.

Mrs. Reagan leaned back, smiling again.

"I thought so. I heard Moon and Dutch talking about you just this morning, before they went off to work."

She arched an eyebrow, staring carefully at Jenny. She seemed to be assessing Jenny in a new way, in a new light. Jenny fidgeted in her chair.

"They spoke very highly of you, especially Dutch," she continued. "Seems he's very impressed. And, I can see why, now that I've met you."

"That's kind of you to say, Mrs. Reagan," said Jenny. "You have no idea how much that means to me."

"Will you be staying in Dixon for awhile?" Mrs. Reagan asked. "We must have you over for supper. Sometime real soon."

Jenny felt a warm glow inside from being with this woman, unlike anyone else she had ever known. There was a feeling about her, a way of expression that made her feel like she was in the presence of someone quite special.

"That would be wonderful. But I don't know," said Jenny.

The sight of Scooter's auto coming around the corner

interrupted her. Beverly waved at her in a manner that suggested something of major importance was brewing.

"Hello, Mrs. Reagan," Beverly shouted as the auto stopped in front of the house. "Nice to see you." She added, "Jenny, can we talk with you, please? It's really kind of urgent."

"Hi Beverly and Scooter," said Mrs. Reagan. "Would you like to join us? I was just about to make some ice tea."

"Thank you, Mrs. Reagan. But we just had our fill of lemonade," said Beverly. "You know mom."

Mrs. Reagan nodded to let her know she understood what she meant. She and Jenny both stood.

"Now, don't forget. You're coming for supper, some night soon," said Mrs. Reagan to Jenny. "Don't let time get away from you...."

"I would love to come, Mrs. Reagan," she said. "I just don't know when it would be."

She hurried down the steps, glancing back up at the thin woman on the porch, and then climbed into the back seat of the auto. Scooter pulled away and drove to a small city park three blocks away. He stopped the car and both he and Beverly turned around, their arms on the front seat, staring at Jenny.

Jenny shrugged, frowning faintly.

"What is wrong?" she asked. "Are you both okay?"

"Jenny, we have to talk," said Beverly. "Serious talk, between friends."

"Sure," said Jenny. "Fire away."

There was a brief silence. And then Scooter spoke up.

"Jenny...where are you from? Really?"

"Like I said, Iowa City. Don't you believe me?" she asked, puzzled, looking a Beverly.

"Sure I do, kid," said Beverly. "But...something's just not right."

"That's for sure!" gasped Scooter. "You might get arrested!"

Jenny grinned at the absurdity of the statement, convinced her new friends were teasing her. But the expressions on their faces quickly discharged that notion.

"Arrested! You're kidding! For what?" she asked, leaning forward.

"For paying for two hot dogs with fake money," said Scooter. "That's what!"

Jenny stopped smiling.

"Oh, no!" she gasped. "How is that possible? The professor gave me some money and...."

She reached in her jeans and pulled out the wad of bills. She thumbed through them, looking carefully at them. All she saw were in a series marked 1926. She pulled one out of the stack, then another. Then a third...which was dated 1985.

"Oh, good grief! I must have had some of my own money in the pocket when the professor gave me the pre-1932 bills and I never realized it in the excitement of the trip. How could I make a mistake like this?" she mumbled.

"Jenny, who is this professor? You said something about him last night, just before you fell asleep," said Beverly. "I'm getting very worried about all of this mystery."

"I was so tired," said Jenny nervously. "What else did I say?"

"Something about...time travel!"

Jenny sagged back in her seat, suddenly very weary.

"Where are you really from, Jenny?" Scooter asked again. "You can confide in us, honest you can."

"Jenny, please?" said Beverly, wringing her hands. "I'm starting to get a little scared."

Jenny smiled weakly at them. She leaned forward and placed her hands on each of their arms.

"There's nothing to be scared of, guys," she said softly. "I wouldn't do anything to hurt anybody, much less two people I really care about!"

"But the fake money. How are you going to explain that?" asked Scooter.

"I've got other bills here," she replied. "Good ones. Drive me out to the park, Scooter, please, and I'll just tell Mr. Hey I had a few play bills mixed in. He'll understand."

Beverly gave a big sigh.

"But, everything else. Jenny, where are you really from?" she asked, her voice weary.

Jenny checked her watch and stared at them. She knew she had to confide in them soon, to at least try to explain some of what was happening. She saw how worried they were, and how confusing it must seem to them to have found such a friend and to know so little about her.

"I can only stay here for a few more hours," she said. "I'll tell you everything, tonight at midnight."

Professor Burns and Brock finished eating a dinner of fried

chicken, green beans and mashed potatoes, all bought in a cardboard box from the local grocery store. They stretched out on a park bench, staring out over the Rock River, a common activity for both of them the past three days.

"The hardest part of her trip is about to begin," said the professor.

"Coming back is tougher than going, professor?" asked Brock, turning to look at his boss. "You never told me that."

"Physically, it's easier, Brock, because your body has already been through the experience once," said the professor. "But emotionally — it can be extremely painful. She has no doubt made friendships that she will treasure the rest of her life. But...they are lost friendships. For the most part, she will never see any of them again, in a meaningful way."

"Except one, right, professor?" said Brock, eyeing the old man he had served so well for two decades.

The professor brushed the crumbs from his legs and gazed out over the water.

"Yes, Brock. Except one."

A voice from behind startled them. They turned to see Brad Taylor standing behind them.

"Any news yet from our traveler, Professor Burns?" he asked, a slight smile on his features.

They both stared at him, surprised to see anyone there, let alone him. Brock stood up to his full six foot, three inches height and glowered at the intruder.

"What's your interest in this, mister?" he said in a challenging tone.

"Why, nothing special," said Taylor, holding his hands up, palms out, and taking a backward step. "I'm just concerned for the professor's welfare, is all. It seems he's so preoccupied with all of this that he's neglected his health. Perhaps you should be paying more attention to that, Brock."

Brock moved over to Taylor, confronting him. But the smaller man stood his ground.

"I'm paid to take care of the professor," said Brock. "Your concern is appreciated and duly noted. But it is not necessary."

Taylor stared up at the larger man and shrugged.

"Okay," he said. "Sorry if I offended you."

He backed away slowly, then turned and jogged away. Brock and the professor watched him until he was out of sight.

"It seems to me you were unnecessarily rude to the young man,

Brock," said the professor. "After all, he did help me the other day, in your absence."

Brock was still staring down the pathway where Taylor had disappeared.

"I tell ya, professor, he's up to something," said Brock, shaking his head. "I don't like him."

"But, what possibly could he want from us?" asked the professor, genuinely perplexed. "Who are we to him?"

"That I don't know," said Brock. "But I plan to be on my guard tonight."

At 8 p.m., Dutch, Beverly and Scooter stood at the curb, next to Scooter's auto. They were whispering excitedly, Dutch pacing back and forth nervously in front of the other two.

"I don't know where she went; honest, Dutch," said Beverly, turning her palms up in exasperation. "I haven't seen her since this afternoon, after we picked her up from your house."

"But, where did you guys go?" asked Dutch.

"Out to the park," she said. "To square matters with Mr. Hey."

"Oh, the play money," said Dutch, smiling. "That was funny. I got a big kick out of it when I heard about it."

"Well, I was worried that he might have her arrested, or something," said Beverly. "You know…passing fake money around can be a big deal, from all I've seen and read."

"Mr. Hey wouldn't do anything like that," said Dutch. "He's a nice man. It was just an honest mistake. No harm was done."

Scooter was fidgeting, his mind going at full throttle as he listened to his two friends talk.

"Maybe we'd better go looking for her," he volunteered. "There's not many places she could have gone. She doesn't have access to a car."

Beverly snapped her fingers and smiled.

"Bikes!" she shouted.

"What?" asked Dutch.

"She told me she loves to ride bikes, for relaxation and for exercise," Beverly said. "She can ride them for hours on end, she said. Come on."

They ran to the small garage behind the house, pushed open the thick wooden door and began rummaging in the dark.

"Owww!" shouted Scooter. "What's that rake doing in here?"

112

"It's a garage, Scooter. That's where rakes are kept," laughed Dutch.

"Hey, guys! One of the bikes is missing," said Beverly.

They walked back outside, glancing up and down the street, then at each other.

"Well, let's go find her," said Dutch. "We'll split up. You two search town and I'll go out to the park."

Chapter Nine

Jenny pedaled into the park, perched atop the large, hard seat of the boy's Schwinn bike. It was so radically different from the sleek racing bikes she owned that it was hard to control and difficult to ride. But she had managed, once she was able to adjust to the different way she was forced to sit and lean over the handlebars.

She enjoyed riding through the town at dusk, and out the long road to Lowell Park. It felt good to work her legs so hard. She slipped past the small Lowell Park sign and down along the narrow road leading into the depths of the park. She took the curves fast, her hair flying behind her,

It took ten minutes to go from the top of the park to the basin, down by the bathhouse. She pedaled slowly past the swimming area, now nearly deserted, and down the long stretch of road. Two pickup trucks were parked near the water's edge, but she didn't see any people near them. Apparently, they were out on the river somewhere in a small boat or canoe.

She rode past all the picnic benches and then was in the long, isolated stretch where the professor had brought the transporter three days earlier. She parked the bike near a large tree and walked back into the woods, to where the machine was sitting. She stopped cold when she saw it, the appearance of it snapping her back into reality…or was it away from reality? The past three days, the seventy-plus hours, had been a blur to her. It was very difficult to distinguish reality from dream. She had slept good each of the three nights, but had dreamed so vividly — with visions of Abe Lincoln, marauding Indians, young militia, Moon Reagan, the dance at old Dixon High School…and, of course, Dutch. It did not seem the least bit possible, and yet she was experiencing it all, somehow.

She walked to the transporter and climbed slowly up the steps. She ran her hands slowly over the chair and leaned over to look at the time dial. She checked the dial and then her watch, which read 7:30 p.m. She sighed heavily and sat on the edge of the platform, her head resting in her hands.

"Only a few more hours! It is true — time does fly!" she muttered.

She walked back to the bike and rode it over to the swimming area. She parked it against a tree near the bathhouse and stared out over the gently flowing river. She could see all the way to the other side, where Black Hawk's little camp sat a hundred years earlier. She dropped down to the thick grass and hugged her knees, lost in a whirling motion of images and thoughts from the last three days.

The sound of a car pulling up made her turn. Dutch clamored out and headed for her on the run.

"Jenny, are you okay?" he sputtered, stopping and gaping down at her. "We were worried…."

"I'm sorry, Ron," she said. "I just needed to be alone for a little while."

He nodded, a slow smile working over his features.

"You weren't going to stand me up for that malted, were you?" he asked.

She stood, brushing the grass off her jeans.

"I would never do that," she said. "Never."

"I…I didn't think that you would," he said.

There was an awkward silence as they merely looked at each other.

"The professor said this would be the hardest part," she whispered half aloud.

"What is hard?" he asked.

She smiled wistfully.

"Would you…hug me, Ron…please?" she asked.

"Sure, Jenny," he said.

He wrapped his arms around her shoulders and she leaned into him. She pushed her hands slowly up his back, hugging him tight. She didn't want to ever let go. She shivered suddenly and he looked down at her.

"Are you okay?" he asked gently, pulling back to peer into her eyes.

"I felt a chill," she said. "Did you?"

"No," he chuckled. "It's…about eighty degrees, I think."

"It wasn't that kind of a chill," she said, hugging him again. She laid her head on his chest and he pulled her in tighter. Neither wanted to let go. At last, she pulled away and took his hand. She walked down to the water's edge, Dutch at her side. She looked up at him and took a deep breath. The moment of truth had arrived.

"I have to leave tonight. Late tonight," she said.

"To where?" he asked.

"My home."

"Iowa City?" he asked with a small shrug. "When will you be back?"

"That's…the problem," she whispered. "I can't come back."

"Jenny, that's silly," he said. "Of course, you can come back."

"No, I can't, Ron," she countered. "Please, trust me. I can't come back. Ever."

He dropped her hand and walked to a bench. He turned to her.

"That's just not so, Jenny. I believe anything in life is possible, if you believe in yourself and in life, itself. There is no reason you can't come back to Dixon…if you want to come back bad enough."

She saw a resolve and firmness in him that she had not witnessed before. His jaw was set tight and he was staring straight into her eyes. She saw his conviction, and his strong sense of optimism about all things being possible.

"That's what makes you so special, Ron," she said. "You do believe in life. You do believe you can do anything; it's the legacy your parents have given you, they and your town. You believe in life…and America. Why, you probably even believe you could be president some day."

He shook his head, as if trying to toss the preposterous idea far away.

"I've never even thought of such a thing, Jenny," he said. "Boy, you sure say some of the wildest things. Asking me where I would go if I could travel back in time…what I would say to Abe Lincoln, if I could meet him. Now, you say I could even be president," he chuckled again, smiling at her.

"You could," she exclaimed. "You could be anything, Ronald Reagan. Anything at all."

"Okay," he said, holding up his hands. "I surrender."

"But, so could you, Jennifer Brix. You inspire me. I've never met anyone like you. And I doubt I ever will again."

She hugged him tight again and stifled a tear.

"You will," she whispered, so low that he could not hear. "Her name will be Nancy."

She looked up at him, smiling.

"I think I want my malted now," she said.

Shortly after 10 p.m., Scooter and Beverly pulled up in front of Beverly's house and saw Dutch sitting on the front steps. The dim light from the porch seemed to bathe him with a slight glow. He had his chin in his hands and looked very sad. They hopped out of the car, and walked up to him.

"We looked everywhere," said Beverly. "We couldn't find her...."

"She's inside," said Dutch, motioning behind him to the house. "She wanted to say good-bye to your mother."

"Where was she, Dutch?" Beverly asked.

"At the park. We brought the bike back in the trunk. We even stopped for a quick malted," he said.

"But where is she going at this time of night?" said Beverly. "She can't travel anywhere now. It's too late!"

There was a long silence.

"The way she's travelling, she can," said Scooter.

Beverly turned to him, hands on hips.

"What the heck is that supposed to mean, Scooter?" she asked.

The front door opened and Jenny stepped out of the house. She walked down the steps and hugged Beverly.

"Ron said you were concerned about me, Beverly. I'm sorry if I worried you," she said softly.

"Geez, honey, we thought you had run away, or something," said Beverly in a high-pitched voice, easing her fingers through her hair. She looked very tired.

There was an awkward silence, broken finally by Dutch. He looked up at the other three.

"She says she won't be back, that it's just not possible," he said dourly. "But, I told her anything is possible in life, if you have the courage to believe it is." He sighed.

"I think we are at a stalemate."

"No...no stalemate," Jenny said, standing by him. "We're both right."

She looked at Scooter and Beverly.

"Will you give me a ride?" she asked.

"Where?" responded Beverly, confused.

"Back to Lowell Park," she said.

"Didn't you just come from there?" Beverly asked. "Sure, if that's what you want. But it's so late, Jenny."

Jenny, Scooter and Beverly walked slowly to Scooter's auto. They stopped at the car door and Beverly turned to Dutch, still sitting on the porch steps.

"Dutch...aren't you coming, too?" she asked.

"We've already said our good-byes," he said. "We agreed to... do it this way."

Jenny climbed in the auto, not daring to look back at Dutch. She had gone to Lowell Park by herself to decide whether to stay in 1932 forever, or return to 1990, and her home and family. She had agonized over the decision for two hours before finally making up her mind. Scooter and Beverly got in too, and the auto started to pull away.

"Wait! Stop!" Jenny shouted.

Scooter slammed on the brakes.

"Wha...." he shouted.

Jenny leaped out of the auto and ran to where Ron was sitting. He stood up and she threw her arms around his neck and clung to him for what seemed like an eternity. He hugged her tightly. She whispered into his ear and he nodded solemnly. She let go and backed up, slowly, step by step, unable to take her eyes off him. She climbed back in the auto and it pulled away from the curb and moved down the street. She stared back at Ron standing stiffly in the light from the front porch, until she could no longer see him.

Back in Lowell Park, they left the auto in a small parking area as close to the transporter as she could get. The three of them traipsed through the woods, crunching on branches laying on the ground and stumbling several times. Jenny led the way, with a flashlight taken from Scooter's car.

"I wish I knew what this was all about, Jenny," Beverly moaned. "This is spooky. I've never been out here at this time of night."

"How about the time you and that guy from Ashton were parked in the car and the police...." began Scooter.

"Oh, shut up, Scooter," she muttered. "You'd believe anything, if you believe that stupid story."

They moved around a huge tree and then Jenny stopped. She shined her flashlight on the transporter sitting twenty yards away. Scooter and Beverly both gasped loudly.

"What in heaven's name...." Beverly mumbled, moving close to Jenny, her eyes glued on the transporter. It looked like a wildly-fashioned boat of some kind to her.

"It's a time machine, Beverly," said Jenny.

"Oh, sure it is," grumbled Beverly. "Of course. Look, Jenny... no more kidding around. You said you'd tell us all tonight what is going on."

Scooter spoke up.

"I think she *is* trying to tell us, Beverly," he said, his voice shaking. He was gaping at the machine, unable to look away from it.

"Scoooooterrr! Not you, too," Beverly groaned, hands flying to her face.

"Bev! Scooter!" Jenny said firmly. "This isn't going to be easy. But listen very closely, and just try to believe me, okay?"

They stared at her in the dim glow of the flashlight. Beverly felt a tremor run down her back and she inched closer to Scooter.

"How do I say this?" Jenny sighed. "Look...try to understand what I'm going to say."

She took a deep breath.

"I'm a time traveler. Don't ask me to explain all the details. It would take too long...and you won't believe me at first, anyway." She paused again.

"Not until you see me leave."

"Leave?" Beverly gasped. "On that thing? Where to?"

"To this very same spot," Jenny said with a weak smile. "Only, one small difference — to the year 1990, which is where I came from."

Scooter walked over to the machine, inspecting it closely, bent over and running his hands along it.

"This is a joke, right?" said Beverly. "You and Scooter are teasing me."

"I don't think she's kidding, Beverly," he mumbled, looking back at her.

Beverly glanced at Scooter, frowning.

"Scooter, stop that. This has gone far enough," she said.

Scooter turned to Jenny, a look of awe on his face.

"I think...she's probably telling the truth, Bev," Scooter said, his voice thick with emotion. "As hard as it is to comprehend, it probably...is...or could be...true."

"How would you know?" said Beverly exasperated. "Is time travel one of your new specialties?"

He looked back at Beverly, adjusting his glasses.

"I've always been interested in that sort of thing; you know that," he said. "I've read and appreciated the books of H.G. Wells, Jules Verne, Edgar Rice Burroughs...."

Beverly groaned and turned toward Jenny, a helpless, pained expression on her face.

"I know it's very difficult to accept all of this, Beverly," said Jenny, placing a hand gently on her arm. "When the professor first came to me with the idea, I didn't believe it, either.

"But the world is such a fascinating place, Beverly. Just think of the telephone, so common now. What if someone had told Abe Lincoln that one day he could pick up a little object and say hello, and another person could hear him — way on the other side of the country. Would he have believed you?

"Would you believe me if I said that in 1969 men will walk on the surface of the moon? It's true, Beverly. We have been to the moon. And we now have movie screens in our living rooms, with full color films on every channel. And with a satellite, you can get over one hundred channels...right in your own living room! It's called television, and it has revolutionized society, and not all for the good.

"Just five years ago, Lindbergh flew the Atlantic in thirty-four hours. Now, we have jet planes that can cross the Atlantic Ocean in three hours and...."

Beverly staggered to a tree, leaning against it, a hand on her stomach.

"I...feel faint," she muttered. "Almost sick...."

Scooter rushed to her and helped her to the platform, to sit her down. She sat heavily and then, realizing where she was, leaped up, backing away from it, staring at it just like Black Hawk's warriors had a hundred years, or three days, earlier. Jenny smiled at her with compassion, understanding how confused and stunned she was. Beverly turned to Jenny.

"Jenny...is...is all of this true?" she asked weakly.

Jenny walked to her and gripped her arms with both hands, peering into her eyes.

"Yes, Beverly. It's all true," she said.

"Does Dutch know?" asked Beverly.

"No, he doesn't," Jenny said. "Please don't tell him about any of this. Or anyone else. Let's have it be our secret; just the three of us. Please."

"But...why tell us?" said Beverly.

Jenny hugged her briefly.

"I wanted you to know. You've given me something special and I wanted to give something special to you, in return," she said.

"But what did we give, Jenny?" she asked.

"The most precious of all human gifts," said Jenny. "Unqualified friendship."

Beverly had to cough to clear her throat and knew she was about to cry. Even Scooter looked away for a moment, back at the transporter.

With difficulty, Beverly composed herself.

"But why can't you stay longer?" she asked weakly. "You've only been here for two days."

"Time travel is very difficult," said Jenny. "The professor said a person can only make four trips in a lifetime at intervals of ten years each. And, if you stay longer than eighty hours at one time, you will not be able to return to the time period that you started from. I love it here, in 1932. The world seems so much simpler, and so much happier. But...I would miss so many things if I didn't return. I have to go back. And Ron...I just can't afford to... to... get involved any more than I am, and maybe mess up history."

Beverly hugged Jenny, then pulled back.

"You really fell hard for Dutch, didn't you, kid?" she said.

"Somehow, I think I have always loved him, in some faraway, remote way," Jenny said. "And then, to actually meet him, here... now...like this...."

"You said eighty hours," interrupted Scooter. "You were only here for about forty hours."

"I was also in 1832, for almost forty hours," she said. "An... unplanned excursion."

"Where?" asked Scooter.

"Right here, Scooter," she said. "With Abe Lincoln, during the Black Hawk War."

Beverly shrieked.

"Now I am going to faint," she said, sagging against Scooter. He wrapped an arm around her, but kept staring at Jenny, a glow in his eyes.

"Do you want to see it work?" Jenny finally asked, to break the tension as much as anything. She had glanced at her watch and saw it was now eleven p.m. She had less than two hours to leave safely and she was now anxious to depart — to escape the overwhelming emotion of the moment and to flee back to the security of her own place in time.

"Yes! Very much so!" gasped Scooter, taking his arm from Beverly so quickly that she almost fell sideways. "Yes!"

Jenny moved to Beverly and hugged her, then walked to Scooter, looking up into his eyes. She hugged him, too. She climbed onto the platform and sat in the chair. She strapped on the belt around her waist and fiddled with the dial. After several moments, she looked up at them.

"I love you both," she said. "We've only known each other for a very short time, but I've never had better friends. Never. Please, don't forget that."

Beverly tried to talk, but couldn't. Scooter wrapped an arm around her again, watching the machine intently. Jenny gazed at them and then turned to face the dial. She turned it on and the transporter began to whir. Beverly gasped, swooning into Scooter's arms, watching through her hands over her eyes. The machine began to quiver. Jenny smiled at them and then waved forlornly. The transporter glowed brightly, began to fade...and then disappeared from sight.

Beverly and Scooter stood alone in the dark, the flashlight shining up from the ground, where Jenny had laid it. Beverly looked up at Scooter and began to cry softly. Scooter gaped, amazed. He eased himself from Beverly's grip and moved to where the transporter had sat seconds earlier, shuffling his feet through the grass.

"Absolutely incredible!" he mumbled. "Unbelievable!"

Beverly came to his side and clutched his arm.

"Please, Scooter, take me home," she whispered, "before I faint."

Chapter Ten

In the dead of night, the professor and Brock waited nervously by the truck. The professor checked his watch time and again.

"She's cutting it close," he mumbled to Brock.

"She still has almost two hours," said Brock. "That's plenty of time, isn't it?"

"Not if something goes wrong," said the professor. "What if she miscalculates. What if...."

A sudden whirring noise stopped him before he could say another word. He and Brock stood mesmerized as the transporter began to materialize out of the dark night. The noise grew, until the time machine became clearly visible. They could see Jennifer in the seat, her head slumped to the side. The machine stopped and they rushed to her. Jenny blinked heavily, then opened her eyes.

"Jenny! Are you all right, girl?" demanded the professor.

She stared at them both, in a daze, and then smiled weakly. She unhooked the belt and stepped cautiously off the platform. They walked with her to the truck, one on each side, touching her elbows gently. She stopped and leaned against the side of the truck.

"Tell me; I must know," said the professor. "How was it, travelling through time?"

She stared at him with a mixture of relief at being back and a sudden sense of sadness.

"It was…just like you said, Professor," she breathed. "In every way. Even the part about being so tired. It's much worse than jet lag."

The professor sighed and sat on the edge of the tailgate of the truck. He nodded his head several times, smiling and staring at Jenny.

"I'm so proud of you, Jenny," he said. "So very proud. I can't wait to hear all the details. But you need rest...."

A crackling noise behind them gave them a start. They all turned and stared into the trees. Brock moved toward the trees, tense and alert and disappeared into the woods. Moments later, the sounds of a scuffle erupted. Jenny and the professor stared helplessly. Finally, all was quiet.

"Brock. Brock? Answer me!" shouted the professor.

Two men man stepped out of the woods, the one in front holding a nightstick in his hand.

"You!" gasped the professor.

Brad Taylor walked toward them, a grimace on his face. He was still in jogging shorts and a tee shirt. The man behind him was covered with sweat and grass stains, and was breathing heavily.

"Brock will be all right, in a few minutes," said Taylor. "He didn't even see the blow coming," he added, tapping the club on his open palm. "He jumped Joe here and got him down and they wrestled around some before I got in a clean shot with the club just as Brock was standing up. He went down hard, but he'll be okay, after a few minutes of head rubbing."

The professor backed up against the truck, eyes narrowing.

"What do you want? We have nothing for you," he mumbled.

Taylor turned from the professor, toward Jenny, and smiled at her.

"This is our traveler, I presume," he said. "Welcome back from the past, Jenny."

Jenny looked at him with a puzzled expression.

"Do I know you?" she asked, shaking from both the strain of the trip in the transporter and a sense of apprehension over this stunning development.

"Hardly. But I know who you are, Jenny," he said. "And I want the blue stone you are carrying."

Jenny was shocked. She hadn't thought about the stone for some time.

"The…blue stone?" she blurted out. "Why…how…."
Taylor walked up to her and held out his hand.
"Yes, if you please," he said sternly.
She stood transfixed, unmoving. He pushed his hand out further and held it in front of her. Finally, she stuck her hand into her pocket and pulled out the stone. She handed it to him and he took it eagerly, turning it over in his hand and admiring it as though it was pure gold.
"But…why? And how did you know about it?" she asked, unable to fathom how he could have known about the stone, and why he would have any interest in it.
Pleased with it, he stuck it into a pouch he was carrying. He assessed her for a moment, glanced over at the professor, then back at her.
"I'm part Sac and Fox, Jenny," he said. "A direct descendent of Black Hawk."
Jenny gasped.
The professor came up to them, his sense of curiosity overcoming his trepidation.
"Will someone kindly tell me what is going on here?" he pleaded.
Taylor started to leave, then turned back to face them.
"I guess there's no harm in that," he said "Jenny is a legend in Sac and Fox folklore. Black Hawk told the story for years, until his death in 1838, of the mystery woman who came into his life and then disappeared in a magic chariot of some sort. He also told of giving her the sacred blue rock, so that she could bestow magical powers on it and bless his people. You might say it is the Rosetta Stone of our people."
"The Rosetta Stone? You know your history, young man," said the professor.
"I should," said Taylor. "I majored in history at Colorado State University. I had you for one course there, in the 1970s."
"But…how did you know I would be going back in time?" asked Jenny. "You couldn't have known about that, if the professor didn't tell you."
"Lots of research, digging…and some blind luck," said Taylor. "I came across a story in an old issue of the Dixon Telegraph newspaper, from the 1960s. It talked about Beverly Grant, who told about a mystery woman she met in 1932. She said the woman claimed to have been a time traveler. Of course, the writer

made fun of it all. But I began to link the story to tales of our tribe, handed down for nearly one hundred and fifty years.

"Beverly Grant said the woman had come from Iowa City in the summer of 1990. So, I have been hanging around Iowa City all year, waiting for the right clues. When Professor Burns showed up on campus, I remembered one remark he made about time travel back in our class at Colorado State. I knew he felt it was entirely possible. So, we followed you here and we have been waiting for you to show up again, from your grand trip. Tonight, our patience was rewarded."

"So, what are you going to do with the stone? Sell it?" she asked, showing a frown of disapproval.

"Hardly," he said. "It is a priceless relic, from a bygone era. It is part of our heritage, part of who we are as a nation, as a people. I will take it to the top tribal elder, who will make the decision on where it will go."

A sudden thrashing noise behind them drew their attention and they turned to see Brock stumble out of the forest, holding his head and groaning. His shirt was torn in front and grass stained. When he saw Taylor and the other man, he shouted a warning and lifted his fists, advancing warily.

"It's okay, Brock! It's okay!" said the professor, moving between them.

"I owe this guy a whacking; he jumped me from behind," growled Brock, looking at Taylor. "I had this other clown under control when...pow! And I'm out!"

"I have what I came for. I don't want any more trouble," said Taylor, retreating quickly.

There was a long, tense moment of silence as the three of them eyed Taylor, and he them. The other man stood behind Taylor, glancing nervously at Brock.

"What do you say, Jenny?" asked the professor at last, turning to her. "You are the one who brought it back. Is the stone his...or is it yours?"

She shrugged, her hands falling to her side.

"As far as I am concerned, it belongs to the Sac and Fox. I want them to have it," she said.

Taylor smiled at her.

"Thank you, Jenny. Black Hawk can rest easy now," he said. He walked a few steps away, then turned back to face her one last time.

"You may be interested to know that Black Hawk had a special name for you," Taylor said. "Roughly translated, it means, 'Beautiful magic woman…who runs like the wind.'"

Jenny sighed as the two men disappeared into the night.

Twelve hours later, a motorboat raced by on the Rock River, pulling two skiers. One of them fell, creating a big splash. The professor and Jenny watched dispassionately from a picnic table bench as the boat circled by to pick up the downed skier. Several jet skis sped by as the downed skier climbed into the boat.

After the incident with Taylor, they had gone back to the motel the professor and Brock had been staying at for the last several days. Jenny was afraid she wouldn't be able to fall to sleep despite being so weary, but she had slept as soundly as she could remember in months. They arose late, had breakfast at a local restaurant and then drove back to Lowell Park, all in relative silence. The professor knew Jenny needed time alone with her thoughts and her emotions; he, in turn, desired quiet time for reflection, as well. And Brock was still angry over the scuffle the night before; he was keeping an eye out for Taylor's return, though he could not come up with any good reason why he expected to see Taylor again, other than Brock wanted to even the score.

"Was it all that you had dreamed it would be…traveling in time?" the professor asked Jenny finally as they relaxed on the picnic table bench.

She reflected for a long time before responding.

"Yes. And more," she said quietly. "But there is great pain, too. You meet these wonderful people, who you care so very much about. And then — poof — they are gone out of your life. Forever. It is too painful for me to cope with…to think I will never see Abe, or Ezra, or Beverly or Scooter ever again. Or see Ronald Reagan as he was in the summer of 1932. So handsome, so full of life…so wonderful." Her voice trailed off.

"But, you can't dwell on that aspect of it," the professor replied. "Concentrate only on the good portion. You had an incredible opportunity to meet two of the most popular and powerful men in American history, in their youth. The very best we have to offer as a nation; it is up to you to use that experience in a way that will make life better and more meaningful…for you. Your life has been enriched beyond measure.

"In addition, their lives were enriched by knowing you," he added, patting her hand.

She nodded at his words. Then she turned to him, staring deeply into his eyes.

"But I still can't figure out why you selected me to go back, Professor Burns," she said. "It just doesn't make any sense at all. All I did was hold your hand...."

He shifted, turning to face her, his eyes glistening.

"Oh, no, Jenny," he said with deep emotion. "You did much more than that. You are the only reason that I was able to develop the transporter."

She was stunned, reeling back.

"Me! But how?" she stammered. "I don't have the foggiest idea of what you mean, Professor. I really don't."

Their eyes were locked tight.

"You've never asked me where I am from," he said, his voice trembling. "But I will tell you this. As a young boy, back in Dixon, Illinois...I rode a scooter everywhere I went."

Jenny gasped, throwing her hands up to her face. She stared wide-eyed at the professor for long moments.

"Oh, my God! I can see it now in your eyes," she croaked. "You...are Scooter!"

"Charles Michael Burns...now known as Professor Burns to some, but once known...as Scooter," he said, his voice low and composed, a trace of pride surfacing in it.

She was shocked beyond words, staring at the professor with tear-filled eyes.

"But...but when did you learn about time travel? And how to build the time transporter?" she asked when she had recovered her voice.

"I learned it was possible...when a girl from 1990 visited Dixon, way back in 1932," he said.

Her head was reeling from what she was hearing and she struggled to comprehend the magnitude of it all. Her chest felt tight, and it unnerved her.

"But...you're the one who sent me, in 1990," she gasped, hands resting on her chest.

"After you left, in that very special summer of 1932, I spent the next forty years of my life, from 1932 to 1970, studying physics, aerodynamics and time," he explained. "I knew time travel was possible because of your visit. And so, I was determined to find the formula. Once I found the formula, I traveled in time myself. And then I came to Iowa City, to find you."

There was a long moment of silence as she tried to digest what she had just been told.

"As a reward?" she asked.

"In a way," he said. "But also as an insurance policy. To insure that you would go back to 1932, to serve as the inspiration I needed. And also so I could view the transporter first hand, in 1932."

"But, if I hadn't gone back, you...you...wouldn't have known...."

"Jenny, who knows what came first, the chicken or the egg?" he said. "If I hadn't sent you back to 1932, I wouldn't have had the opportunity to see the transporter and I might never have devoted my life to it and time travel. Also, if I had not done that, you couldn't have gone back.

"I am both the chicken and the egg, it seems," he said with a wry smile. "I sent you back in time so that I could learn from you how to go back in time...and yet I was able to send you back only because you had already traveled in time! If I hadn't invented the time transporter, I probably would have married Beverly...and spent the rest of my life in Dixon."

She was shocked again.

"You didn't marry Beverly?" she asked. "Why not?"

"Oh, no; I never married," he explained. "I became so captivated by history and time travel that I devoted my entire life to their study. I left Dixon soon after you did and spent twelve years at various colleges, earning a total of six degrees. Then, I journeyed all around the globe, tracking down any small lead I could find that might relate to time travel. You know, we are not the first to travel in time, you and I. It is being done, albeit on a very limited basis, by others."

"Who?" she asked. "My god, that's incredible!"

"I can't say yet. But it will come to light soon enough, when the time is right," he said. "It will cause...an explosion of both shock and re-evaluation around the world."

"Whatever happened to Beverly?" Jenny mumbled. "She was such a wonderful girl."

"She married a school teacher and they moved to Arizona," he said. "I haven't seen her for many years."

"To...think...I was just with her a few hours ago," she said softly. "My goodness."

Jenny walked to a tree, leaning against it, her eyes on the gently-flowing Rock River. It reminded her of Time itself.... the way it continued on its slow but methodical journey, nothing able to deter it or stand in its way. The professor followed her and stood beside her, watching her with great pride and affection. She was like the daughter he never had.

"How come I went first to 1832, instead of 1932?" she asked. "Was that a mistake, or did you do that on purpose?"

"That was an honest mistake, Jenny. I must have moved the dial when the deer startled me. A freak accident on the trek through Time. Maybe I had a premonition and that's why I gave you the piece of paper at the last second, to remind you of how to adjust the time dial. I don't know for certain. But what a wonderful side trip, meeting Abraham Lincoln and Black Hawk." He paused, shaking his head.

"But I have a question for you, Jenny. It's been haunting me. That last night...when I stopped the car; I've often wondered what you said to Dutch when you jumped out and ran back to him that night, fifty-eight years ago!"

"Fifty-eight years ago?" she gasped. "It seems like only yesterday." She paused and sighed.

"I told him two things; to please never forget the way America was then, in 1932 Dixon. People full of pride, love, and full of respect for one another. Those qualities are what makes America so great, and so prosperous.

"And then — I told him that I loved him, and that one day he would make all of Dixon very, very proud of him."

Professor Charles Michael "Scooter" Burns smiled at her and wrapped an arm around her shoulder. She leaned into him and hugged him tight, tears rolling down both their cheeks.

Chapter Eleven

The day started out with a drizzle, but by late afternoon the sun had come out and the temperature was in the mid eighties. Thousands of spectators lined the road winding through the bottom part of Lowell Park. They stood six and seven deep, for half a mile. The small motorcade wound through the park, ten cars in all. Former President Ronald Reagan rode in the third car back. An aide sat next to him, smiling but watching the crowd intently. Secret service men were all around.

Tom Sharp, a television announcer from station WOC-Davenport, was one of a dozen reporters on hand; he felt a special pride, knowing that Dutch Reagan had once worked at his company back in the 1930s, when it was only a radio station. He stood with microphone in hand as technicians fluttered around him, making sure everything was ready for the big moment. Finally, he received his cue.

"It's a magnificent day, in all respects," he began, smiling into the camera. "And Dixon has turned out in full bloom to greet its favorite son, Ronald Reagan. This is a special trip for Mr. Reagan, a trip dripping with nostalgia. The president has said on numerous occasions that many of his happiest memories are of his lifeguard days at Lowell Park. He was a lifeguard here for seven summers, from 1926 through 1932. And, he is credited with saving seventy-seven lives during that time. He certainly cut a dashing figure, back then as lifeguard. Some experts say this photo of lifeguard Ronald is the most widely-seen of any photo ever taken of a United States president. And it was taken right here in Lowell Park, over sixty years ago."

He paused while the camera focused on the photo of Dutch Reagan as a Lowell Park lifeguard, then he turned, eyes wide.

"Here comes the president's car now," Sharp said in a hushed voice. "He is in a convertible. We are told that Mr. Reagan insisted, despite the protests of the Secret Service, to be in a convertible so he could get a really good look at the people and the spot that he loves so much...this great reminder of his youth.

"For all we know, at his age, this could be the President's final trip to Lowell Park."

The caravan wound slowly through the park, a stream of black and gray cars. Reagan wore a light blue suit and sat tall, waving in response to the enthusiastic greeting. As the applause grew and grew, he stood and smiled, very appreciative of the response.

Suddenly, he stopped waving....the smile fading from his face. He stared hard at a certain spot. His hand moved to his chest, gripping it.

"What is it, Mr. President!" shouted his aide, jumping up to grab his arm. Two Secret Service men leaped into action, running to his side, hands on their revolvers, staring out into the crowd. The president sagged back into his seat, still gripping his chest, his face ashen white, the aide bending over him. The caravan came to halt, the people gaping, confused and frightened.

"What's wrong? What happened?" dozens asked, staring about in every direction.

Jenny stood by a large tree, knowing full well what had taken place. When she heard that Ron was coming back to Dixon, for a final visit, and would be driving through Lowell Park, she knew she simply had to come, she simply had to be there. She arrived early and sat waiting for two hours, watching the people streaming in and listening to the excitement build. She glanced continuously at the old bathhouse, now empty and forgotten, and at the spot in the river where the slide had thrilled thousands of youngsters, summer after summer, for decades. The emotions became so overpowering that she had to fight the urge to leave the park; but when she saw the caravan coming her way she was thankful she had stayed. She leaned against the tree, near the very spot where she had last been with Dutch, sixty-two years earlier. She had stared at his approaching car, a lump growing in her throat.

Her heart pounded as she saw him stand, waving, smiling...so happy to be back in Lowell Park. And then his eyes fell on her, and she saw the startled look on his face. She felt a stab of anxiety race through her entire body as he gasped and then slumped back into his seat.

"Mr. President! Mr. President!" shouted his aide, the others hovering nearby. "What happened, sir? Are you okay?"

Dutch stared forward and caught his breath. Then he turned and climbed back to his feet. He looked over at the tree, but Jenny was gone. He searched the crowd for her, but she was nowhere to be seen.

"Mr. President!" the aide croaked again.

"Yes, yes. I'm okay," Dutch said. "I thought...I thought I saw someone; someone from long, long ago who came into my life only for a very short, wonderful spell. But, now I don't see her." He looked around again and began to wave faintly at the crowd. They waved back, relieved.

"Maybe I was only dreaming — one last time," he said half aloud.

As the procession started up again, Ronald Reagan glanced back over his shoulder, at the very special spot he had shared with Jenny Brix for a very brief moment in 1932. And then he sighed and turned away. Behind him, Jenny Brix stood alone behind the tree, overwhelmed by memories of days long gone.

Postscript

Charles Russell Lowell bought the three hundred or so acres known as Lowell Park in 1859. A native of Massachusetts, he planned to live on the land some day. But while fighting on the Union side during the Civil War, he was killed in the battle of Cedar Creek, Virginia, on October 19, 1864. He was twenty-nine years of age. His wife, Josephine Shaw Lowell, died on October 12, 1905, in New York and shortly after their daughter gave the land to the City of Dixon, on behalf of her parents.

Today, the City of Dixon has several powerful reminders of the legacy of two of the nation's most respected and beloved Presidents. In a small park in the center of town, between the two bridges spanning the Rock River, the only known statue of Abe Lincoln as a soldier in the Black Hawk War overlooks the river. The statue at 100 Lincoln Statue Drive was dedicated in 1930 by the State of Illinois and sits on the original site of the blockhouse known in the mid-1800s as Fort Dixon. The little area is called President's Park.

The Ronald Reagan Boyhood Home at 816 S. Hennepin Avenue was the first home the Reagans lived in when they arrived in Dixon in 1920. It entertains some 12,000 visitors a year and is on the National Register of Historic Homes. Four blocks north, at the corner of Hennepin and 5th Street, sits the large brick building once known as South Side School. It is where Dutch attended school and graduated from in 1928. It has been restored and is now a research facility called the Dixon Historic Center.

When Dutch came home in the summer of 1932 to work his final summer at Lowell Park, the family was renting a small house on Monroe Avenue. That house no longer exists.

Just a few miles north of Dixon, on the east side of the Rock River across from the city of Oregon, a huge statue of Black Hawk stands on a bluff overlooking the river. The massive sculpture, depicting the famous warrior with arms folded and wrapped in a blanket, stands nearly fifty feet tall and can be seen from a considerable distance along Route 2, on the west side of the river. The statue is the work of well-known artist Lorado Taft and was erected in 1910.

In 1997, the bathhouse that Dutch Reagan used as a lifeguard in the summer of 1932, and in six previous summers, was restored through the efforts of the Dixon Area Chamber of Commerce and various community members. The project culminated a long effort to keep the building from being razed.

In various letters through the years, Ronald Reagan has reflected on his days at Lowell Park with great fondness. Below are excerpts from three such letters.

• A March 4, 1947, letter written to Mrs. Alvah Drew of Dixon bears a return address of Warner Brothers Studio, Hollywood, California. In the letter, Reagan mentions "time" once and refers twice to Lowell Park:

"I'm not going to remark how many years ago all those Dixon days were because some how they seem much too close and fresh to be tagged with a date. I guess time isn't very important after all because I can remember every knot hole in every plank of the old dock out at Lowell Park." Later, in the same letter, he talks about meeting a Dixonite during World War II: "We had quite a rehash of the summer days at Lowell Park..." He signed the letter "Best to you, Dutch."

Mrs. Alvah Drew's maiden name was Elizabeth "Bee" Frey. She was a member of the Dixon High School class of 1927, one year ahead of Reagan in school. In the summer of 1927, she took the photo of Lowell Park lifeguard Ronald Reagan that appears on the cover of this book.

• In 1973, Governor Reagan wrote to a former Sunday school teacher in Dixon about the impact of the summers spent in his hometown. "Every once in a while I pinch myself sitting opposite the head of state of one or other of the dozen nations we've visited, thinking this can't be 'Dutch' Reagan here. I should still be out on the dock at Lowell Park."

• Perhaps his most melancholy reference to his Lowell Park days came in a letter he wrote to a friend with the nickname of Light, written prior to running for governor.

"Just a hasty note to return your letter – I hope it will never appear in your scrapbook as from a man who became pres.

"I'm still mulling the Calif. gov. thing with no answer as yet but have a feeling they are closing in on me.

"Whatever happened to laying in the sun at Lowell Park? — Best, Dutch."

About the Author

In 2002, Mike Chapman retired from a 35-year career as a newspaper editor, writer and publisher, including ten years as executive editor of The Telegraph in Dixon, Illinois. During the Dixon period, he and his wife, Bev, and three children lived just one-half mile from Lowell Park and visited it frequently. He met Ronald Reagan on October 30, 1990, when the former President returned to Dixon for the final time. Mr. Chapman considers meeting Ronald "Dutch" Reagan one of the highlights of his life. *Lowell Park* is his fifteenth book.